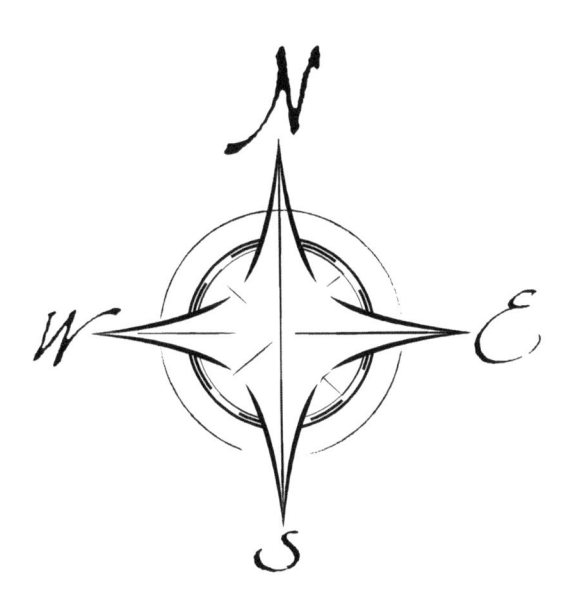

The Four Corners
of Winter

SHINE-A-LIGHT
PRESS

Visit Shine-A-Light Press on our website:
    www.ShineALightPress.com
    on X: @SALPress

Visit The Four Corners of Winter on our website:
    www.TheFourCornersBooks.com
    on X: @4CornersTrilogy

Visit C.S. Elston on his website:
    www.cselston.com
    on X: @cselston

The Shine-A-Light Press logo is a trademark of Shine-A-Light Corp.

The Four Corners of Winter
    Copyright © 2024 by Christopher Scott Elston

All rights reserved. Published by Shine-A-Light Press. Shine-A-Light Press and associated logos are trademarks and/or are registered trademarks of Shine-A-Light Corp. No part of this publication may be reproduced, stored in a retrieval system, or transmitted in any form or by any means, electronic, mechanical, photocopying, recording, or otherwise without written permission of Shine-A-Light Corp. For information regarding permission, please contact the permissions department at www.shinealightcorp.com.

Publisher's Note: *The Four Corners of Winter* is a work of fiction. Where real people, events, establishments, organizations, or locales appear, they are used fictitiously. All other elements of the novel are drawn from the author's imagination and any resemblance to actual persons or events is coincidental.

Scripture quotations are taken from *The Holy Bible, New International Version ®, NIV ®*,
 Copyright © 1973, 1978, 1984, 2011 by Biblica, Inc. ®. Used by permission. All rights reserved worldwide.

Illustrations by Madison McClean

Author's Photo by Christie Bruno

ISBN: 978-1-953158-23-9

Printed in the U.S.A.

For the McClean "kids" who have grown up to be some of the best adults I know. Being your "Uncle Crispy" is one of my life's biggest blessings.

Among them, I have to single out "Maddie Cakes" whose talents know no bounds. Her illustrations for this book series not only made it better, but I will forever cherish the fact that we were able to collaborate in this way, starting when she was so young.

All four of you add joy to my life. Thank you.

Acknowledgments

As always, I would like to extend my deepest gratitude to my original proofreaders: My parents, Doug and Judy, and my wife and editor, Andrea. They have all been supportive in numerous ways, not the least of which is having read drafts of the book before publication and offering valuable feedback.

I also want to acknowledge A. Brekke, who is the first person I know of to describe the Aurora as "curtains."

I would like to further offer a sincere 'thank you' to my niece, Madison McClean, for once again providing her beautiful artwork for the interior of this book. I appreciate the hard work and feel grateful for the opportunity to share it with everyone who reads this book.

Table of Contents

Part One *Thanksgiving*
Chapter One – *Break* 3-9

Chapter Two – *Hungry* 11-16

Chapter Three – *Family* 17-22

Chapter Four – *Transition* 23-28

Part Two *Familiar*
Chapter Five – *Kinship* 33-37

Chapter Six – *Signs* 39-45

Chapter Seven – *Christmas Eve* 47-52

Chapter Eight – *Duty Calls* 53-56

Chapter Nine – *Exit* 57-61

Part Three *Unfamiliar*
Chapter Ten – *Cold and Lonely* 65-71

Chapter Eleven – *Shelter* 73-80

Chapter Twelve – *Herd and Seen* 81-87

Part Four *Searching*
Chapter Thirteen – *Wranglers* 91-98

Chapter Fourteen – *Seeking Unity* 99-104

Chapter Fifteen – *Smoke* 105-111

Chapter Sixteen – *Poof* 113-119

Part Five *Polarized*
Chapter Seventeen – *Split* 123-131

Chapter Eighteen – *The Longest Day; Even Longer Night* 133-140

Chapter Nineteen – *The Door Closes* 141-147

Part Six *The Final Quest Begins*
Chapter Twenty – *White on White*   151-157

Chapter Twenty-One – *Seeing Red*   159-165

Chapter Twenty-Two – *Partaking*   167-173

Chapter Twenty-Three – *Forging Ahead...While Possible*   175-181

Part Seven *Hurdles*
Chapter Twenty-Four – *Mood Swings*   185-192

Chapter Twenty-Five – *All Who Wander*   193-199

Chapter Twenty-Six – *Partly Cloudy*   201-207

Part Eight *Ice Walkers*
Chapter Twenty-Seven – *Glass*   211-218

Chapter Twenty-Eight – *Subzero*   219-226

Chapter Twenty-Nine – *Soul Survivors*   227-234

Part Nine *From Cold to Hot*
Chapter Thirty – *Steam*   239-245

Chapter Thirty-One – *Unstable*   247-254

Chapter Thirty-Two – *Heat*   255-260

Chapter Thirty-Three – *Hell Spawn*   261-266

Chapter Thirty-Four – *Heaven Scent*   267-271

Part Ten *The Last Battle*
Chapter Thirty-Five – *Tarry*   275-281

Chapter Thirty-Six – *Legions*   283-288

Chapter Thirty-Seven – *The Word*   289-295

Chapter Thirty-Eight – *Return*   297-301

Reader's Guide Pages 306-308

The Four Corners
of Winter

by C.S. Elston

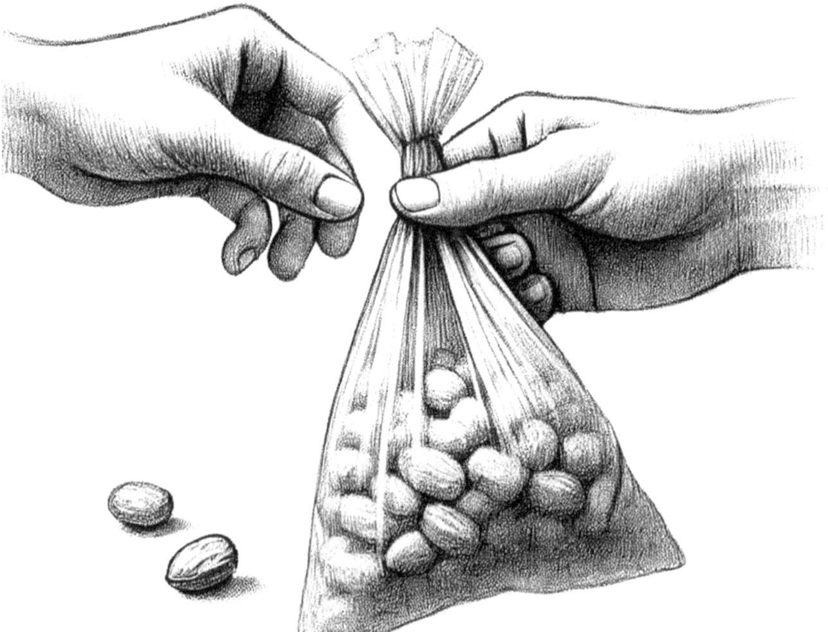

PART ONE
Thanksgiving

CHAPTER ONE
Break

"Hey, good day?" Tatum asked as her little brother, Kinsey, climbed up and into the front seat of her 1998, pink Jeep Wrangler Sahara. It had been lifted four inches higher than the factory position to accommodate the oversized tires. Kinsey closed the door before buckling his seatbelt.

"Awesome," he quickly responded. "At lunch, Adam burped so loud it startled Chelsea Longhorn, who was at the table in front of us, and when she jumped, she spilled the milk she was drinking down her shirt, in her lap, and some of it even came out of her nose. It was hilarious!"

"Probably not for Chelsea," Tatum responded sincerely but with a small chuckle as she put her Jeep into gear and pulled out of her space in the high school's student parking lot. "How embarrassing."

"Yeah," Kinsey agreed, "but still hilarious. Even Chelsea was laughing about it."

"That's good. Still, poor thing. So, you ready for Joe Flows?"

"Definitely. I've been ready for my Bullinger since about 11:30 this morning."

"It's like forty-two degrees outside. Why can't you order something hot like a normal human being?"

"I like the Bullinger, regardless of the temperature. Besides, we're going to be sitting inside where it's warm. What difference does the outdoor temperature make?"

"Okay," Tatum conceded as she stopped her Jeep at a crosswalk before turning left, "that's a pretty decent point. What's in those things, anyway?"

"Mostly Red Bull, but I think there's also some lime juice and ginger beer."

"I do like ginger beer, but I'll take my extra hot almond latte and sit by the fireplace so I can get cozy."

"And you think I'm crazy?" Kinsey asked, looking over at his sister with a grin forming on his face.

"I know you're crazy," she teased back.

The pink Jeep meandered through Snohomish, Washington until finally coming to a stop and parking on the south side of Second Street in front of a barbecue restaurant, just two doors down from Joe Flows. Tatum and Kinsey climbed out, walked to the coffee shop where Tatum worked on Saturdays and, true to their word, ordered a medium almond latte and a large Bullinger. She sat by the fireplace, warming herself with her back to the flames, and Kinsey sat directly across from her with only a small table between them. They enjoyed their drinks and talked more about their separate days at school.

It was a routine that had started shortly after Tatum got her driver's license more than a year earlier. Kinsey had expressed disappointment that their walks were going to come to an end before she even had her learner's permit. But this new tradition that replaced the walks had so far satisfied that concern and would continue to do so, at least until the end of the current school year.

"Are you still thinking Biola for college?" Kinsey asked with a hint of sadness in his voice.

"Depends on scholarships," Tatum responded thoughtfully. "That school's crazy expensive."

"Mom and Dad want you there as bad as you do. They'll find a way to make it work even if they're keeping it to themselves so you'll push harder for the scholarship money. Trust me, you'll be just fine."

"It would be nice to get some California sun. Spend some time in Uncle Ray's old stomping grounds. Check out some of the places he's made legendary, like that donut place."

"Sidecar."

"Exactly. He's made me want to try that so bad."

"Me, too."

They shared a smile, but Tatum could tell what was really on Kinsey's mind. "It'll be weird at first, but you'll be driving yourself soon after I'm gone. Then you can come here with your friends. Start a new tradition."

"I don't know. I'll find something else to do with them. I think I'd rather save this for us. We can do this whenever you come home on breaks."

They shared another smile before Tatum decided to change the subject. "Are you excited about your first year of high school track?"

"Yeah," Kinsey quickly responded. "I don't expect to make varsity or anything, but hopefully training with the older kids will help get me ready by next year or at least the year after that."

"I think you'll do better than you realize."

"I guess we'll find out in a few months."

"I guess we will."

"So," Kinsey started with a bit of a thoughtful pause, "if you go to Biola next year, you'll be like a thousand miles away."

"True," Tatum responded with equal thoughtfulness, "but it's less than a three-hour plane ride."

"Right, but how often do you think you'll make that plane ride?"

"Well, it's not like I can come home on normal weekends, but I'll be back three or four times a year for at least a week or so with things like spring break. Christmas is longer, and summer is, well, a lot like our summers now. Plus, you can always come visit me down there, too. Biola is inland, but we can still go to the beach, maybe even learn to surf. And, who knows, if we time it with Uncle Ray visiting his family, maybe he can show us around Long Beach."

"Sidecar," they said in unison.

"Jinx," Kinsey quickly added. "You owe me a Bullinger."

"I already bought you a Bullinger."

"You owe me another one."

"Nope. All paid up."

"Fine," Kinsey yielded with a smile. "That does sound fun. Cali, I mean," he added while letting his smile grow.

"It does, doesn't it? What do you say we finish our drinks in the car. I'm sure Mom's scrambling to get ready for Thanksgiving dinner tomorrow. We should probably get home and help."

"Let's do it."

The short drive involved a lot less conversation. As soon as Tatum started the engine, they turned the radio on instead. She had developed a taste for country music because of her dad, Grant. But it was a little more "current" than his and wasn't limited just to country. In fact, on that last stretch, it was Lauren

Daigle that was singing them home. Kinsey was fine with it, too. Although he had his own favorite artists like TobyMac, Skillet, and NEEDTOBREATHE, he also looked up to his big sister and thought that anything she liked simply had to be cool.

Just after the pink Jeep, with its black hardtop and black tire cover on the back spare that had the iconic Jeep headlights and grill in perfectly matching pink, came to a stop in its usual spot on the far-left side of the Snyder's driveway, Kinsey and Tatum both hopped out. They quickly reached back inside for their school bags, shut their doors nearly simultaneously, walked to the front door, and stepped inside.

The siblings were immediately approached by their mom, Jill, who excitedly told them to remove their shoes and take everything to their room. They did as they were instructed, and when they were walking back down the stairs to the entryway, she next advised them not to enter the living room because she had already vacuumed it and didn't want to have to do it twice.

"Mom," Kinsey started with a little confusion as they stopped at the bottom of the stairs on the same rug where they had been standing only a minute earlier, "nobody's going to be here for twenty-four hours."

"Yes," Jill agreed but not without qualification, "and there's a lot to do in those twenty-four hours, which means I don't have time to do things twice. And don't think I'm not about to put you two to work."

"We know," Tatum stated a bit defensively, "that's why we're home a little earlier than normal."

"Good," Jill said with a smile before turning and hustling off, expecting them to fall in line, "I need you both in the kitchen."

"Are we supposed to follow her?" Kinsey quietly asked.

"I think so," Tatum stated as if there was a hint of uncertainty even though there really wasn't any at all.

"I vote we go the other direction. I have a feeling I'm going to need another Bullinger."

"I think I'll join you this time but make mine a double."

CHAPTER TWO
Hungry

Jill and Tatum were up until after midnight baking three pies: apple, pumpkin, and pecan. Grant and Kinsey, on the other hand, had both fallen asleep watching the University of Washington men's basketball team beat South Dakota State. Or at least they hoped that's how it had ended up. The Huskies had a twelve-point lead when Grant conked out, and by the time Kinsey joined his dad in slumberland, the lead had increased to eighteen. The boys didn't wake up until the girls came in and gave them a shake. They had considered banging some pots and pans together to startle them, but truth was, they were too tired to take the loud noise themselves. Everyone stumbled up the stairs and performed an abbreviated version of their bedtime routine. Kinsey didn't even get through half of the eleventh chapter of the book of Hebrews before he was done for the night.

He woke up with his reading light still on at 7:24 a.m. His

tummy growled. *Thanksgiving*, he instantly thought as the corners of his mouth turned up and his eyes began adjusting to the light. Springing out of bed with an enthusiasm that caused him to temporarily forget his morning Bible reading routine, Kinsey swung his door open, and the wonderful smells filled his nostrils. There were still leftover scents from making the pie the night before, and he knew they would soon be mixed with the turkey which would be placed in the oven to start baking in a couple of hours. Kinsey looked back in the room at his clock and felt his tummy growl again. His mom never let anyone eat anything on Thanksgiving until company arrived about an hour before dinner was served. The meal was scheduled for just over seven hours from then, and he didn't know how he was going to make it that long without devouring something.

Used to Kinsey's annual complaining, Jill tried to keep him busy with chores. Putting him in charge of mashed potatoes seemed like particularly cruel and unusual punishment for a crime he didn't even commit. The football games on the TV were a welcome distraction, but they were professional teams, and Kinsey preferred college. He had inherited that trait from his dad. The Huskies wouldn't play until the next day. It was the Apple Cup, the game when they played their biggest rivals, the Cougars, every year. That would be a fun one to watch, but it was something else he had to wait for. Between the Apple Cup the next day and the delicious dinner an ample number of hours away, that dawn to dark's life-education theme was clearly patience, and Kinsey was feeling like a slow learner.

Tatum had an easier time when it came to the patience aspect of that particular day. For one thing, she rarely woke up hungry, and today was no exception. In fact, Tatum typically didn't eat much at breakfast time unless it was a sweet treat like a cranberry-orange scone or pancakes. So, the time she had to spend anxiously waiting for dinner would be significantly shorter. The Apple Cup, on the other hand, was something she was really looking forward to. That event would stretch her patience elasticity more than anything else she was anticipating.

Jill was too busy to concern herself with anything but having the house clean and decorated, as well as, arguably most important, the dinner done on time shortly after their guests arrived. Neither hunger nor football were anywhere near her thoughts. Of course, it didn't hurt that she allowed herself to taste-test things as she cooked.

Grant was the one who had the day the most figured out. College football was never on Thanksgiving, so he had accepted that a while back. It had taken him longer, but he had recently learned that when Jill sent him to the grocery store for pre-meal snacks like nuts and crackers, he bought double the amount on her list so he could nibble on them without risking upsetting her by eating something she was planning on using. So far, she was not even aware of his extra purchases, but Grant had convinced himself that if she ever needed more than she had planned on, that was a scenario he could come out of looking like a true hero. Unless, of course, he had already eaten the spare supplies by then. It was a possibility that grew stronger with each passing hour.

Not surprisingly, by the time the clock struck noon, he was working with a dwindling supply of mixed nuts as he snacked on them while raking the leaves in the front yard; a process that was taking longer than Grant thought it should, due to the occasional gust of wind that was redistributing his nice, neat piles. At first, he tried to chase and catch the scattering leaves but quickly realized the process was futile. Instead, he chose to stand patiently, waiting for the wind to die back down before raking the leaves up again and trying to scoop them into the yard waste bin prior to the next gust. The waiting slowly evolved into an excuse to take a break and eat a few more nuts.

Quickly scrunching the bag up and shoving it into the pocket of his jacket, Grant scrambled to chew as fast as possible and hide his secret activities as the front door swung open and he expected to see Jill standing on the other side of it. Instead, Kinsey moped down the steps and approached him grumpily.

"Dad," he started with an annoyed tone to his voice, "Mom won't let me eat anything. Nothing. She's starving me to death."

"I hardly think she's starving you," Grant stated through a mouth-full of nut-crumbs.

"Hey," Kinsey fired back as he noticed the words his dad was using sounded like they crawled through a wind-tunnel full of debris, "what are you munching on?"

Grant put his right hand on Kinsey's back and slowly turned him, matching his own maneuver, so that they were both soon facing away from the house, making it look suspiciously like some illegal activity was taking place between father and son in the Snyder's front yard. "I might know of a way I can help," he finally stated with his teeth clenched like a bad ventriloquist. Kinsey looked up at his dad, eyebrows furrowed, in total confusion. "Don't look at me," Grant nervously stated.

"Why-"

"Just act normal," Grant jumped in, cutting his son off.

"This is far from normal," Kinsey said quietly.

"Do you want the stuff or not?"

"What stuff?" Kinsey asked sincerely.

Grant looked around, including behind him, to make sure they weren't being watched. Slowly, he pulled the bag of nuts out from his pocket, but only halfway. It was just enough to give Kinsey a glimpse and let him know what he was offering. Kinsey's eyes quickly went wide with desire as Grant shoved the bag back into his pocket and looked around again.

"You want it?"

"Oh," Kinsey said with a drawn-out moan, "I want it alright. I want it bad."

"Then be cool," Grant insisted. "Just be cool, man."

"I'm cool... Hungry, but cool."

"You have to keep this to yourself."

"I'm not exactly in a sharing mood."

"Good," Grant said as he continued to swivel his head and make sure no one had started to watch them. "Let's keep it that way."

Kinsey's mouth watered. He licked his lips as Grant pulled the bag back out of his pocket and quickly handed it to his son. "You just saved my life," Kinsey said as he took the bag, opened it, and shoved his hand inside. He raised a handful of nuts to his mouth and smiled at it. "Mom tried to take it away and you saved it."

Grant watched his son start chewing with intense relief and knew, right at that moment, that his bag of nuts was as good as gone.

CHAPTER THREE
Family

"Mom!" Kinsey yelled from a standing position in front of the big window in the living room which looked out at the front yard. "The Schoens are here!" Kinsey loved his mom's sister, her husband, and all five of their kids, who each happened to be younger than he was, but he was mostly excited that the painful wait for food was almost over. The agony could have been much worse if his dad hadn't shared his secret stash of nuts with him, but the aroma of cooking turkey now filled the house in such an inviting way that the anticipation remained nearly unbearable.

Once the greetings were over, his boy cousins were quickly asking to go outside and toss the football. Kinsey made them wait a couple of minutes while he scarfed down some tortilla chips covered in hot, spinach-artichoke dip before finally accommodating them with a game of "Flyer's Up" that ultimately led to yet another game. This time it was "Two-Hand-Touch" football.

The kids were in the front yard, and therefore the first to greet new arrivals, as Jill's other two sisters and their families showed up. All the girls and the adults went inside while the boys stayed out. The one exception was Ray. He remained outside and became the permanent quarterback for both teams until the call came for dinner. It wasn't that he was uncomfortable going inside. This was his second Snyder Thanksgiving, after all. He simply enjoyed activity, and throwing a ball around was more exciting to him than anything that could be going on inside the house.

The other men were watching football on the television, although the older girls had convinced them to switch over to the parade during commercial breaks, while the younger girls were up in Tatum's room, playing with her old dolls and going through her closet as they talked about how "cool" her clothes were.

Finally, the call came, and Kinsey thought that meant it was time to eat. Unfortunately, he would have to wait a little longer because his mom decided to start a new tradition. As the family gathered in a circle to pray before the feast, she wanted to have every person there quickly tell the group what they were thankful for. Kinsey could see the turkey on the counter, although it was still on the roasting rack and tented in tin foil waiting for Grant to carve it. Nevertheless, it was taunting him and torturing his tastebuds from inside its temporary hiding place. Even more, he was mentally drooling over the thought of his mom's sweet potato casserole hitting his tongue. As most of the youngest kids delayed things by showing their shyness and indecision, the anticipation was excruciating. But, attempting to keep his impatience under wraps, he waited and declared his thankfulness like everyone else.

The general consensus, particularly among the Snyders, was a genuine thankfulness for family. It was a theme of gratitude that had become exponentially more important to them since their first trip to Kadosh five years earlier; a lifechanging event that was extremely difficult but even more rewarding. It had given them a perspective on their lives, past, present, and eternal, that they wouldn't trade for anything.

With the new Thanksgiving tradition complete, Grant prayed for the meal and then everyone took their seats and started loading up their plates. Kinsey quickly ran out of room and boasted that he would be going for round two in ten minutes or less. He dumped enough gravy over his potatoes and turkey to force his black pepper flakes into a breaststroke and then dove in with extreme enthusiasm. Truth is, it was closer to fifteen minutes before he reloaded his plate with sweet potato casserole, intentionally placing it where his roasted Brussels sprouts had been in an unsuccessful attempt to avoid the leftover gravy puddles, but he did go for a round two that was about half the size of round one. And then… He was stuffed, much like the turkey had been. By the time people started slicing up the pies, Kinsey was done with putting food in his mouth. He decided that the sweet potato casserole had been his dessert and told his sister that he was already starting to look forward to making sandwiches out of the leftovers at lunchtime the next day. She shook her head with a grin, amazed by her little brother's obsession with food.

Other than Jill's sisters, who had kicked her out of her own kitchen and announced that they were on clean-up duty, everyone found a spot to watch football after dinner. The activity that came before the meal was complete, and the entire group was predominantly motionless. Kinsey was almost over capacity, full to a slightly painful degree, but still managed a contented smile as he closed his eyes and drifted off to sleep.

Grant was only minutes behind his son on naptime, but both Jill and Tatum stayed awake; Jill to keep her conversation with Ray going that had started at the dinner table, and Tatum to watch the Cowboys squeak out a win over the Commanders.

Ray was the last one to leave, and that was on purpose. He wanted to talk to the Snyders about Kadosh. Out of everyone who had been in attendance, they were the only five who had any experience with it. The Snyders had shared it with the family and some friends over the years and received diverse responses. Some were skeptical, unsure of what to believe, if anything at all, while others were fascinated and wanted to hear every detail. But, in any case, no one who hadn't been there could truly, fully understand what they had been through. So, in most settings, it had become easier to not bring it up in mixed company.

"Any word on the final return?" Ray casually asked, causing everyone to look at Kinsey who simply shook his head, indicating he didn't know anything new.

"Well," Ray started back in, "I've been praying about it a lot since we got back and…" Ray sighed before continuing, "I'm not feeling the pull this time. I think my time in Kadosh is already over. So, when you do get the call, I think you'll be headed back there without me this go 'round."

After a brief moment of surprised quiet, Grant spoke for the group. "We understand, but we'll miss you."

"Thanks," Ray responded. "In a strange way, I'll miss being there. I hope this doesn't sound like a cop-out, but when I pray, I feel like I'm being told that you've been called back but I haven't. Kind of humbling, actually. My ego wants to be part of it, but my ego isn't calling the shots."

"Can't argue with that," Jill chimed in. "It doesn't sound like a cop-out at all."

"I'm a little jealous," Tatum admitted. "I kind of wish we

didn't have to go back. Kadosh is never easy."

"True," Kinsey agreed. "But, when duty calls, we'll have to answer."

"Know this," Ray announced, "no one will be praying for you guys harder than I will be."

"We know," Jill said with a smile.

They truly appreciated the support, and they were all praying about the events to come, too. But the painful truth was, while they knew they would be going, they didn't know when, and like Kinsey's hunger, the anticipation was extremely difficult. Sometimes the gap between awareness and performance, or prayer and answer, is just as important as the events that bookend it. This was no different. God was giving the Snyders exactly what they would need to get through the difficult journey that lay ahead. He was filling them up with time together in order to combat the time they would soon have to spend apart.

CHAPTER FOUR
Transition

No one in the Snyder house was more excited to decorate for Christmas than Tatum. She was up and out of bed before 7:00 a.m. on Friday, the day after Thanksgiving, which was early for a non-school or church day, and in the attic removing boxes less than fifteen minutes later. Unfortunately for Grant and Jill, the door to the attic wasn't your typical ceiling one in the garage or the hallway. It was a miniature door in the wall at the back of their long and narrow, bedroom closet. Tatum had once commented to Kinsey that she figured it was about half the size of what she imagined a hobbit's door in the Shire would be if they could visit Middle Earth.

The kids had loved playing in that attic while growing up. It was the most common spot to conceal themselves during games of hide-and-go-seek. It had plywood flooring that made it look like it was still under construction, and one overhead light that only illuminated about half of the extensive room. Full of boxes, luggage, and Tatum's old, yellow and white dollhouse that was as big as an ATV, there were countless places to hunker down while the seeker was on the prowl.

Kinsey even had a few sleepovers in the attic before his family began to separate themselves, especially in an emotional way, and Kinsey had withdrawn from both his parents and his friends. Thankfully, their first trip to Kadosh had changed all of that, and when they returned, they grew closer than ever. Kinsey had also re-entered the world of friendships. By then, however, he had grown up a little and decided not to return to the attic sleepovers.

The maturing young man was the last one to get up that morning. Not because he didn't enjoy decorating for Christmas, but because his room was the furthest away from the noise that his sister was making. All that racket had meant Grant and Jill were awake shortly after Tatum had gotten started and hearing every move their daughter made on the other side of their closet wall.

By 8:00 a.m., the entire family was sipping either coffee or hot chocolate, working together downstairs with Christmas music filling the air, and pulling both indoor and outdoor decorations from the boxes they had retrieved out of the attic.

The Four Corners of Winter

Grant had been resistant to a fake Christmas tree until the previous year when a bug infestation that resulted from his real tree caused Jill and the kids to gang up on him and force him to buy one on a giant discount after the holiday. This was going to be the first year the Snyders would be without a real tree. But even Grant agreed, once it was up, that the fake tree looked both real and beautiful. Only half joking, Grant had, in preparation for the day, purchased a few pine tree air fresheners from a local car wash and hung them as the first ornaments to make the real-looking, fake tree, smell about as real as an overwhelming, artificial pine scent could make it.

There was always a bit of lighthearted debate about which Christmas song was best. Grant had settled on For King and Country's version of "The Little Drummer Boy" because he loved the pounding drumbeat, while Jill had gone deep into her recesses and pulled out her mom's favorite "Come on, Ring those Bells" by Evie because it took her back to her childhood. Tatum was happy with anything from Alan Jackson's *Let it Be Christmas* album. Kinsey, who typically took a significant portion of his music cues from his dad and sister's country tastes, and a fair amount of both newer and classic rock'n'roll tunes, had a more surprising choice. He favored both the songs *O Holy Night* and *Silent Night* and didn't really care who was singing them. It could be Sarah McLachlan, Nat King Cole, Mariah Carey, or Percy

Sledge. It didn't matter. Those songs always made him stop and ponder the importance of the holiday.

Next up were the outside lights. The Snyders weren't attempting to win any contests, and certainly weren't trying to rival the Griswalds in Grant's favorite Christmas movie, but they weren't holding back either. They trimmed the house lines, the two big windows on the front, and the door frame in white, covered a half a dozen bushes and two trees in green, and those same tree trunks were wrapped in blue lights to honor the Seattle Seahawks. Grant would have preferred to honor the Huskies, but purple lights had proven too difficult to find. The final touch outside was an eight-foot tall, prefabricated "Star of Bethlehem" that they put on their roof. Back inside, there were a lot of knick-knacks and things they put out, too. And finally, the stockings were hung from the fireplace mantle to make the Snyder house at Christmas feel complete.

It was a two-day event, and by Saturday night they were all pretty wiped out. But, as had become custom, they sat and watched the original *Home Alone* movie which Grant and Jill had been excited to introduce their kids to a number of years earlier. They had eventually watched all the sequels and spin-offs, too, but nothing compared to the original. It was their clear family favorite, making everyone teary when the neighbor, Marley, got a visit from his son and his son's family, and the single movie that had become the standing tradition.

Each weekend that followed, someone got to choose their personal favorite Christmas movie, and the family would watch together. This meant, when it was Grant's turn, *National Lampoon's Christmas Vacation* was on. Kinsey was almost as predictable; he nearly always chose *Elf*. Tatum had learned that if she wanted to avoid groans and complaints about it not being a real Christmas movie from her brother and dad, she shouldn't pick *Little Women*, but that didn't always mean they were safe. When they were, she had them watching either *The Santa Clause* or *Fred Claus*. Jill took her choice old school. Way old school. She went with either *It's a Wonderful Life* or the original *Miracle on 34th Street*. Even though everyone picked their own favorites, they all enjoyed watching the movies again. Even Grant and Kinsey secretly enjoyed *Little Women*. But most of all, they enjoyed the fact that they were establishing traditions as a family.

Among them were the bowls of homemade popcorn they had on each movie night. As they sat down to watch *Home Alone*, it was the first thing they had eaten since Thursday night that wasn't made up of remains from that big meal. The food had mostly been sandwiches and various side dishes. Some sandwiches were open faced with turkey, mashed potatoes, and gravy. Others were turkey with mayonnaise and mustard. They all had one thing besides their composition of leftovers in common though: deliciousness.

The next day was a typical Sunday. After showers and a small breakfast tide over, the family went to church together. The sermon was fittingly on being thankful, and the capper was a Peter Kreeft quote, "Thanksgiving comes after Christmas," which appropriately bridged the gap between the two holidays while completely flipping the calendar around. It caused a lot of thought-provoking conversation amongst the Snyders on the car ride home, including Grant's point that, technically and historically, the first Thanksgiving came way after the first Christmas. They all accepted that fact but decided that wasn't the point of the quote.

Ultimately, they were all in one accord with the opinion that they were now full steam ahead in the holiday season that made them the most thankful: the season that celebrated the incarnation and proved that God loves us so much that He humbled Himself to the point of becoming a man, destined to be the sacrifice necessary to cleanse us of our sins. They all agreed that there simply was not anything to be more thankful for than the amazing truth of Christmas.

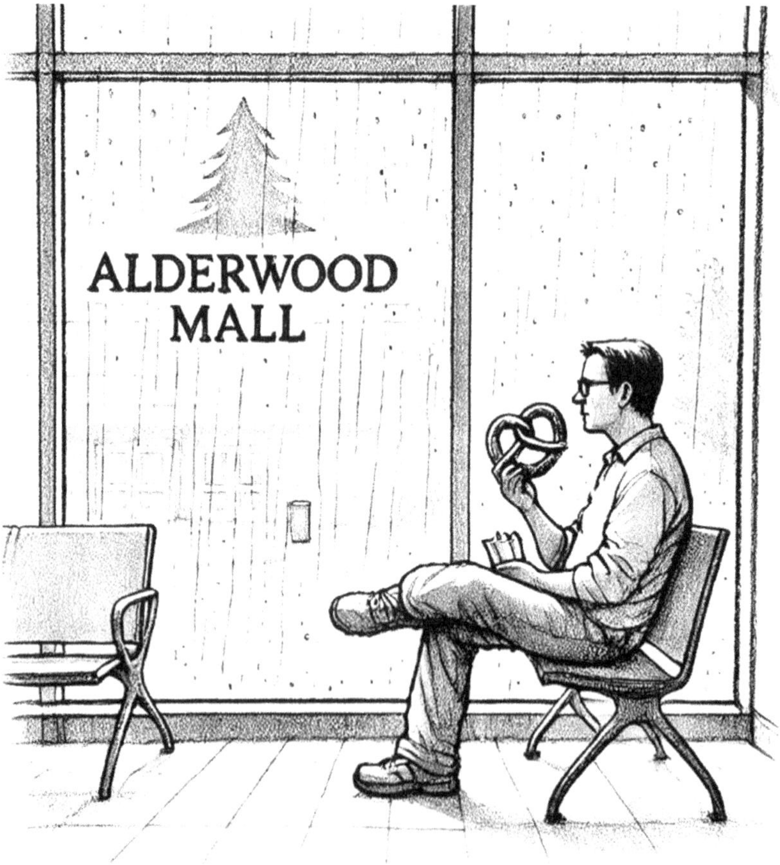
ALDERWOOD
MALL

PART TWO
Familiar

CHAPTER FIVE
Kinship

Since they last returned from Kadosh, the Snyders had begun to seek others out who had had a similar experience. It started when Grant, on a whim, typed the word Kadosh into a search engine. At first, he saw what he expected to see, and it confirmed what Kinsey had learned on their first trip to the islands. Kadosh was a Hebrew word that meant "set apart." But a deeper dive showed that the type of set apart that the word referred to was that of being sacred or designated for a holy purpose. Grant had never thought about it in that way. He had only thought of it as his family being separated from one another. It had conjured up negative connotations, but that clearly wasn't the original definition of the word. *Leave it to the enemy to take something God intended for good and use it for his evil purpose instead,* Grant considered. *Good thing God can flip that around; take what the enemy intends for evil and use it for good.* His thought process continued as he reflected on what Kadosh had done to restore his family to the tight-knit unit God always meant for it to be. Furthermore, the experience had brought them to God, Himself. *What an amazing blessing.*

However, as the rabbit trail continued, he also learned Kadosh was the title of an Israeli film that had played at the Cannes Film Festival a couple of decades earlier, the title of many songs, even someone's last name, and that a "Knight Kadosh" was what they called a Freemasonic initiation ceremony. So, while Grant had not been familiar with the word before his entire family had been pulled out of their world and sucked into the one ruled by Raum, he was finally accepting that it was far more common than he had previously known.

It was a search Grant found himself going back to with increasing frequency. Each time he did, he scrolled through more and more pages of things he had already seen in order to ultimately get to the new stuff. A few months down the road, he finally hit on something that grabbed his attention like an oncoming freight train. It was a posting on some obscure social media platform called "thalk," and the note by someone with the handle KYFamilyMan simply asked the question,

> Has anyone out there ever been to a place called Kadosh or heard of someone from there named Raum?

Grant felt his entire body sit back a few inches, then he leaned in close and read it again. He had known in his heart since their first return that others had returned, too, and that they must be out there, but this was the first proof he had seen. He went to the site, hoping to respond to the guy, but quickly discovered he needed to set up an account. He felt awkward and a little gun-shy about using his real identity for fear of people thinking he'd lost his mind, so he set up a new email address and used it to register for an account on the platform. He continued to aim for anonymity, so in both places, he simply called himself Kadosh Survivor.

Able to see more with a registered account, he noticed that the posting was over a year old and quickly confirmed that no one had responded to it in that time. He wasn't sure why, but he found it difficult to come up with the right words to say. He went back and forth, typing and then deleting, but ultimately settled on a reply far shorter than the allotment from the platform:

Yes. What island were you on?

After submitting, Grant just stared at it for a while. He knew it was silly to expect an immediate response, but he couldn't help himself. It was torture as he checked back almost constantly while he ended up waiting for several days before KYFamilyMan finally answered. But once he did, it was with a great deal of enthusiasm, and the aftermath of that Band-Aid being ripped off was an onslaught of communication that came several times every day.

It turned out they had been on the same island and knew each other quite well. It was Qasim, one of the two men who had given Grant a place to sleep in their hut on his last trip to Kadosh. At first, they were just thrilled to reconnect. They caught up on what had gone on at home since getting back, including Qasim's family immigrating from Morocco to Bowling Green, Kentucky. Eventually, their conversation turned to the idea of searching for other people from Kadosh.

They started reaching out on additional social media platforms and slowly put together a private, world-wide support group. While the two of them were about 2,500 miles apart, they were both able to find people much closer to each of them, and families with this common experience started gathering to encourage one another. They met for coffee, shared meals, and had barbecues that were like Kadoshian family reunions.

It was a good thing, too. Grant was surprised to learn that some people had convinced themselves their trip to Kadosh wasn't even real. There were those who had decided it had to have been a dream, even when they had learned that they had shared it with other family members. Some had hidden it entirely because they thought they were going crazy. Most, however, knew it was real but, like the Snyders, had primarily been keeping it to themselves for fear of the reaction from those who could never understand what they had been through. It was a therapeutic endeavor for a lot of people who desperately needed it.

Almost unanimously, particularly once the mental and emotional healing had taken place, survivors agreed that Kadosh had changed their lives for the better. Yet, when the Snyders brought up the idea of a return trip down the line, everyone quickly refuted the concept. They said it sounded too scary, too dangerous, and too risky. They had made it out once but didn't want to press their luck a second time around.

While the entire family continued to try and find new survivors, and even recruit them for an eventual return, it slowly became clear that, while it resulted in a comfort at home, when it was time for their final return to Kadosh, the Snyders would be going alone.

CHAPTER SIX
Signs

The Alderwood Mall in Lynnwood, Washington had been a staple in the Snyder household since even before the family truly began. The mall opened in 1979 when Grant and Jill were barely out of diapers. They had spent time there when they were dating and seen it go through a lot of renovations over the years. The kids had been raised going to the mall for back-to-school shopping, to get their picture taken with Santa Claus, to watch movies, and just like they were doing on this particular day, to buy each other Christmas gifts. They had split up and intentionally gone to different parts of the mall to ensure their purchases remained a surprise.

Tatum was on the first floor of Nordstrom hunting for a present for her dad in the men's department. She had looked at ties, sweaters, and button-down shirts, but couldn't find anything that she was excited about and also fit the "fifty dollars or less" budget restriction she had placed on all of her gifts that year to help her start saving a little spending money to take with her when she eventually went to college.

As she slowly turned in a circle hoping to spot more options, she began to take notice of the loud and repetitive pounding noise she was unexpectedly hearing. She looked up to where the sound seemed to be coming from but saw only the ceiling. She then glanced over to the large glass doors that led out to the parking lot. That's when she noticed how dark it was outside and that it was pouring down rain, which she didn't remember being in the weather forecast. The Northwest is known for precipitation so that wasn't surprising, but the heaviness and volume of this rainfall was unusual.

~

Jill's mind quickly drifted back to her last trip to Kadosh. Shortly after arriving, she had found herself in a dark forest. She had just banged her knee on a fallen tree when a similarly heavy rain had begun to fall. The lonely, frightened feeling she had experienced then suddenly returned to the pit of her stomach. Jill did not want to admit it to anyone, but she really had no desire to go back there. After all, the life she was living at that moment truly was a happy one.

She figured, since God already knew, she could at least confess her misgivings to Him and ask for the peace that only He could provide anyway. Briefly closing her eyes in the middle of Forever 21, she did exactly that.

~

Grant reopened his eyes and took a bite of his Auntie Anne's pretzel. He looked down at it and wondered how soon he'd be stuck in Kadosh with food he had to catch, cook, and find a way to flavor with none of the conveniences of a modern American kitchen. He expected the peace he'd prayed for to come, but he had to admit that it wasn't there yet.

~

While it wasn't typical for Kinsey to be alone in a women's clothing store, he found himself, at that moment, holding a hanger out in front of him that displayed a top he thought his sister would appreciate. He pursed his lips and nodded his approval at no one in particular before turning toward the cash register, ready to make the purchase. As he started to walk, he noticed that the rain shower outside the window was slowing down a bit.

Recollecting his slip and slide down the muddy hill in Kadosh, a grin suddenly crept up in the corners of his mouth as he also recalled meeting Pablo and Caleb for the first time shortly after his body finally came to a stop. *There are good things about Kadosh, too,* he thought. *Good people in a bad spot that need to come home.*

~

Jill's peace began to settle in as she thought about the barbecue they had hosted the previous July and the fact that her Kadoshian friend, Olivia, had brought her entire family, great-grandkids and all. She truly believed that both trips to the strange place had been worth everything they entailed, and she was gaining confidence that a third would be no different.

~

The flickering lights interrupted Grant's thoughts as everyone around him stopped in their tracks and started looking up in wonderment. He took his last bite of pretzel, crumpled up the wrapper, and tossed it in the garbage. *Is the storm causing power issues,* he wondered, *or is this something else?*

The Four Corners of Winter

~

As the lights continued to flicker and the whispers of the people around her turned into chatter interrupted by gasps, Tatum began trying to figure out where her family would be at that moment. They were supposed to all meet up at Panda Express in the food court, but that wasn't for another forty-five minutes. *If Kinsey is shopping for one of my parents, he's either here or at Macy's. If he's shopping for me, he's at Loft. My mom could be anywhere they sell clothes, and my dad is supposed to be shopping but is probably eating either a cookie or a pretzel.*

She looked up the escalator and considered the climb to the other floors of the store. A glance outside showed flashes of lightning, and the sound of thunder that followed caused her to flinch. She then looked out into the main part of the mall and decided that trying to find her dad was her best bet.

~

Kinsey had finished his cash transaction and exited Loft. He passed Eddie Bauer and took a left at the jewelry store. He walked by about another half dozen storefronts before reaching Auntie Anne's, right next to Cinnabon. He looked around and finally spotted a familiar face. His dad was staring up at the lights, which had stopped flickering, as Tatum approached him.

"Hey, kiddo," Grant said as he gave his daughter a side-hug. "Backup generator must've kicked in. Heard some pretty crazy thunder though, huh?"

"Yeah," she responded as Jill walked up behind them, leaned over their shoulders, and put her arms around both of them, "where did this come from? Hey, Mom."

"Hey," Jill responded, "good question."

Kinsey approached, and the family finished off their group hug as everyone around them seemed to go back to what they were doing with little more than a brief experience to talk about.

"I guess it's over," Jill announced as she pointed to the windows by Dave & Buster's. Other than the wet pavement, you would never know that a storm had just been active. The sun was shining, and the sky looked as clear as it had on any day the Snyder's could remember seeing in Washington State at that time of year. "Weird."

"Super weird," Grant admitted.

"You don't think…" Jill started to slowly ask, "it had anything… to do with…"

"No," Grant said, clearly understanding exactly where his wife was going with the question she was trying to get out. "That's too big of a reach, even for Raum and even by Kadoshian standards."

"It wasn't Raum," Kinsey interjected as he pointed to a flashing exit sign. He lowered his arm, turned around to face his family, then lifted his arm again and pointed at another exit sign that was also flashing. They all spun around. Three exit signs were visible, all were blinking, but only the Snyders seemed to be paying any kind of attention.

"Does that mean we're leaving?" Tatum asked.

"Not yet," Kinsey answered. "But soon. Real soon."

CHAPTER SEVEN
Christmas Eve

The day before Christmas had a very specific schedule to it in the Snyder house. It was one that had evolved over the years, but by this point in their lives, it was pretty well locked into place. It started with a rule that everyone got to sleep in. So, as people woke up without an alarm, they had to keep the noise down to let everyone else sleep as long as their bodies would allow. The catch was that whoever slept the longest was responsible for providing breakfast for the rest of the family. It was their choice whether they went out and bought it or stayed home and cooked it themselves, but it couldn't be something as simple as a bowl, a spoon, a carton of milk, and a box of cereal. It had to be unanimously considered a proper breakfast that required some real effort on the part of the provider. It also made the morning a mystery which was part of the fun.

Kinsey was the big "winner" that year, and he made a large batch of scrambled eggs for the family. He never made the same scramble twice because what was in it always depended on what was in the fridge. He often incorporated leftovers, and that morning was no exception. The Snyders had tacos a couple of nights earlier, so Kinsey added some taco meat, ranch dressing, salsa, cheddar cheese, pinto beans, and green onions. He also made home fries with potatoes, butter, onions, and a variety of seasonings as a side dish. Grant announced that he thought it was their first Mexican Christmas Eve breakfast. Jill added that it might also be their best. Grant and Tatum agreed.

When the late meal was over and the kitchen had been cleaned up, it was time to watch some college football and start slowly getting ready to go to Jill's sister's house for an early dinner and present exchange. The gathering consisted mostly of the same group that had been at the Snyders' for Thanksgiving, but Ray wasn't there because he had flown to California to be with his family. The adults didn't exchange gifts with one another, but they got one for each of the kids. It was a lot of fun and a lot of noise. The evening was also a pot-luck style dinner. Jill's middle-sister's contribution always depended on which fad-diet she was trying that season. This was the year she went gluten-free and offered up some "pizza bites" that included a crust that seemed to take four or five times longer to chew than it should have.

Lucky for her, she had plenty of leftovers that everyone insisted she take back with her.

Before returning home, the Snyders attended a Christmas Eve candlelight service at their church. The key verses their pastor referenced were John 1:1-5, 14:

> In the beginning was the Word, and the Word was with God, and the Word was God. He was with God in the beginning. Through him all things were made; without him nothing was made that has been made. In him was life, and that life was the light of all mankind. The light shines in the darkness, and the darkness has not overcome it. The Word became flesh and made his dwelling among us. We have seen his glory, the glory of the one and only Son, who came from the Father, full of grace and truth.

Kinsey fixated on the light versus dark part of the passage as he thought back to their last trip to Kadosh. They had been in the dark until the light showed up on Raum's island and chased the darkness away. He couldn't help but smile at what an amazing thing the presence of God really was. Continuing to listen, he heard the pastor as he preached on those verses for about a half an hour and then summed everything up with two quotes from C.S. Lewis' book *Miracles*:

> "The central miracle asserted by Christians is the Incarnation. They say that God became Man. Every other miracle prepares for this, or exhibits this, or results from this."

> "In the Christian story God descends to re-ascend. He comes down; down from the heights of absolute being into time and space, down into humanity . . . But He goes down to come up again and bring the ruined world up with Him . . ."

The Snyders all went away overwhelmed by the warmth of God's love, not just for them but for all of creation. They knew, too, that they were among the blessed few who had felt that warmth physically on Raum's island in the middle of Kadosh on both of their trips to that strange world. It was that warmth, that presence, that made Kinsey smile in the middle of the sermon, and it brought a similar smile to everyone's face on the car ride home. The possibility of feeling that amazing warmth again was one of the very limited number of things that excited them about going back.

The final tradition on the schedule for the Snyder Christmas Eve was the opening of a single present by each family member. They drew names from a bag to determine who each person was getting a gift from and then pulled the present that matched the draw from underneath the tree. They also opened them in reverse order of age which meant Kinsey got to go first.

He drew his dad's name and was handed a rectangular box that had been wrapped, but not with his mom's usual precision, so he knew this had truly come from Grant. He ripped the paper off and quickly lifted the top from the box to reveal a pair of black hurdle shoes that he immediately knew would go well with his track uniform. Tucked into the heel on the inside of one of the shoes was a bag of metal spikes that screwed into the bottoms. He jumped up and gave his dad a big hug and said his thanks before sitting back down to handle the shoes while he watched Tatum unwrap her present from him.

Kinsey was by far the worst in the family at wrapping presents. They were always overdone with too much paper, which made them poofy instead of tight and clean. This was no exception. In fact, it was probably the worst presentation of any gift Kinsey had ever given. But, as Tatum unwrapped it, it became clear why that was the case. He had rolled a large blanket and wrapped it without a box. While the presentation of the gift itself was horrible, the blanket was a pretty, teal-colored, polyester fleece material with the words *faith, hope,* and *love* written in white. Tatum immediately enveloped herself in it and told Kinsey how cozy it was. He said it was meant for their movie nights, but she could also take it to college with her. They exchanged hugs and thanks, much like Kinsey had already done with his dad, and then sat back down for the part they were both most excited for.

While Jill had drawn Tatum's name, and Grant had drawn Jill's, they made a special exception to the rules to account for the fact that the kids had teamed up to give their parents a single present. Jill's gift to Grant would have to wait until morning since the "one gift each" rule was not negotiable.

Kinsey had saved up as much as he could, but Tatum had pitched in more than half because she was the one with a job. They handed over a simple envelope, and after a little gushing, Jill opened it to find a gift certificate to a bed and breakfast in Langley, Washington, where two college kids had spent a weekend between their sophomore and junior years after getting married, for a short honeymoon. Since then, they had also discovered a restaurant in nearby Freeland that had become their absolute favorite "anniversary spot," so the possibility of going there immediately sprang to their mind as well.

Grant and Jill stared at the gift certificate for a moment, looked at each other, then at their kids, and tears formed in their eyes at the thoughtfulness and the realization of just how far they had come. Not just in their marriage as a whole since those college days, but specifically as a family since their first trip to Kadosh. It was a tender moment for all four of them.

They would be thankful for the memory of that moment sooner than they realized because the call for one last trip to that dreary world was approaching quickly.

CHAPTER EIGHT
Duty Calls

It had gotten quite late, and everyone was hustling off to bed. They prepared for slumblerland while looking forward to a morning filled with breakfast casserole, the last day of Christmas music for about eleven months, and of course, both stocking stuffers and additional, bigger presents.

Kinsey brushed his teeth as he pulled down his covers, got his Bible out, laid it next to his pillow, and pushed the switch to turn on his reading lamp. He went back to the bathroom and rinsed out his mouth before saying goodnight to his parents and sister. Finally, he flipped the switch on the wall to turn off the overhead light in his room and closed the door.

As he crawled into bed, Kinsey climbed over his Bible, laid down next to it, pushed his pillow up against the headboard, picked up the only book he had made a habit of reading twice a day, every single day for several years and counting, and opened it to where he had left off that morning before getting up to greet his family. That put him at the beginning of the thirteenth chapter of the Gospel According to Mark where the author was describing the signs of the end of the age and then transitioning into what had come to be known as the abomination of desolation. The part that stood out to Kinsey, and he couldn't be sure why since it was a warning for pregnant women, was the eighteenth and nineteenth verses which read:

> Pray that this will not take place in winter, because those will be days of distress unequaled from the beginning, when God created the world, until now—and never to be equaled again.

Kinsey found himself fixated on that prophetic scripture as his eyes grew tired. He wondered what it was that was tugging at him. The Spirit within him was connecting to the passage, but he couldn't quite make sense of it. As his mind wandered, he thought about what a horrible time it was describing and how awful it sounded to be living in this world during that coming period. His heart grew heavy as he couldn't help but feel sorry for those who would have to endure it.

It was a lousy sentiment to end the day on, but slowly his thoughts faded, and he drifted off to sleep with the lamp still on. And, as he meandered into unconsciousness, the glowing ball from the lamp on the other side of his eyelids diminished nearly into oblivion. But soon, another light appeared inside of it, grew out of it, and then moved toward him at a much faster pace than the previous one had disappeared. It quickly enveloped him in a truly comforting way. It felt familiar, too.

Suddenly, Kinsey remembered having a dream leading up to his last trip to Kadosh. It featured a ball of light that he had looked into, and he had received the identical sensation. He remembered thinking that it was like being tucked into his own bed with a warm blanket.

This was it!

But instead of being something small enough for Kinsey to focus on and look into, this time the light was all around him, making this experience fit the "blanket idea" even better than the last one had. Suddenly, a voice interrupted the moment just as it had previously.

"You knew the time would come," the voice bellowed, "and come it has. The people who remain trapped in Kadosh need you to show them the way out. They are being given a final chance, not because they deserve it, but because the grace of He who sends you demands it."

"I know," Kinsey softly replied as he enjoyed the coziness that covered every inch of him. "I'm ready."

"Gather your family," the voice roared in an authoritative but inviting tone just before the light sped away even faster than it had arrived.

"Wait, don't go!" Kinsey yelled as he sat straight up in bed, suddenly wide awake and already missing the warmth he was enjoying only a moment earlier. He looked down at the Bible in his lap and re-read the verse he had been focused on when falling asleep. It started, "Pray that this will not take place in winter."

Kinsey didn't read any further. He put his Bible down and climbed out of bed. Briefly looking back at it, he considered the possibilities and then walked slowly to the door. He opened it and stepped out into the hallway. Tatum was already standing out there in front of her room.

"I just had the weirdest dream," she whispered. "I was visited by what felt like the light from Raum's island."

"I had it, too." Kinsey and Tatum both looked up, locking eyes for the first time since going to bed.

"So did we," Grant said as he and Jill stepped out of their room.

"It's time to go," Jill added as everyone shared pensive glances with one another.

"Yeah, and I think it's going to be cold," Kinsey announced. "Really, really cold."

CHAPTER NINE
Exit

The Snyders had long since recognized that they couldn't take things with them to Kadosh. Grant had a flashlight in his back pocket when they left the last time, and although he had no recollection of letting it go, it was waiting for him on the ground when they returned. But, on both of their previous trips, the Snyder family had arrived wearing the very same clothing they had on when they departed. With that knowledge, Kinsey's prediction of extreme cold, and the realization that their return to Kadosh was imminent, they found themselves digging through drawers and closets for all the snow gear they could find.

Had they not been so focused on their departure, the activity may have brought back memories of old ski trips up Stevens and Snoqualmie passes to the east of where they lived, north to Mount Baker, or even their solitary trip to Mount Bachelor in

Oregon. But they didn't have time to reminisce. Kadosh was calling, and Kinsey's weather forecast had added a reasonable element of panic.

Once everything was laid out in front of them, they began putting as many of their clothes on themselves as possible. Having decided they could always take clothes off when they got there, this seemed like the safest approach. It started with long underwear and socks, which sounds simple enough, but Grant felt like he needed a giant shoehorn to get into his twelve-year-old underwear bottoms and would probably need a pair of scissors to eventually get back out.

Next were jeans, another layer of socks, and t-shirts. This was all followed by snow pants, glove liners, and sweatshirts. Finally, they added boots, gloves, beanies, and thick, winter coats. Almost immediately, they discovered that their body movement had been seriously impaired. Collectively, they looked like four people of varying sizes all dressed up like Randy Parker in the movie *A Christmas Story*.

They discovered at the top of the staircase, when Grant and Kinsey collided and accidentally formed into what looked like one giant cushion, that two at a time would cause a traffic jam, and they were quickly forced to switch to a single-file line. They marched down the stairs like Imperial Stormtroopers following orders handed down through the autocratic Galactic Empire directly from Emperor Palpatine himself, and collected in a circle in the entry way to the house.

"I guess Christmas will have to wait," Grant stated matter-of-factly.

"Sounds like we're headed to Narnia," Tatum quipped.

"What do you mean?" Jill asked sincerely.

"Where it's always winter," Tatum started to answer but turned to Kinsey to let him finish for her.

"But never Christmas," he stated without missing a beat.

"Of course," Jill acknowledged with a grin.

Grant opened the front door, ushered everyone outside, followed them onto the porch, and closed the door behind him. They began the slow trek into the woods. Had it not been for the swish-swoosh of their loud winter clothing rubbing against itself, the walk would have been performed in complete silence. Grant didn't take a flashlight with him this time, and the difference in visibility was obvious. No one cared, though. They were too preoccupied with the dread that came from knowing they were all about to be split-up and that the time before the reunion they prayed would eventually come was likely going to be lengthy. It would certainly be full of adversity and struggle. Inevitably, they arrived at the spot where all four of them had disappeared and, ultimately, reappeared, twice.

Just as it had previously, the group's collective heartrate

increased substantially. The silence continued as everyone reached out and grabbed one another's hands while forming a circle much like they had in the entryway of their house just moments earlier. They bowed their heads and closed their eyes while Grant began to pray for both wisdom and protection.

Just a couple of sentences into the prayer, they began to feel the familiar warmth surge within them and flow out of every square inch of their bodies. Eyes still closed, their hands gradually released from one another as they felt themselves begin to float off the ground.

~

Tatum steadily became aware of the same rushing sound she remembered hearing at this point of her journey the last time she left for Kadosh. She slowly opened her eyes, excited to see the beautiful colors she also remembered. Immediately, she was pleased to discover that disappointment wasn't going to be an issue as the luminescence came flooding toward her.

~

Kinsey once again took mental note of the steady pulse within the light. He remembered thinking it was like a heartbeat on his last journey, and suddenly the phrase *God is light* came to his mind. He stared in amazement at the awe-inspiring sight before him and wondered if this could be the very Spirit of God, the source of all life, transporting him to Kadosh to complete the task He had called the Snyder family to accomplish.

~

A longing developed inside of Grant as he watched the light begin to fade, and with it, the warm feeling that he had been experiencing since he was in the woods near home. However, as the light was replaced by darkness, another, albeit wholly different light, became visible in the distance. It was like a white line, expanding horizontally into the entire horizon ahead of him and then vertically until no darkness remained. Suddenly, absolutely everything was completely white.

~

As if Kadosh was revealing its current state to her, Jill realized that she had just watched, for the first time, the strange world come into view. Even more startling was the revelation that the entire place was encased in snow and ice.

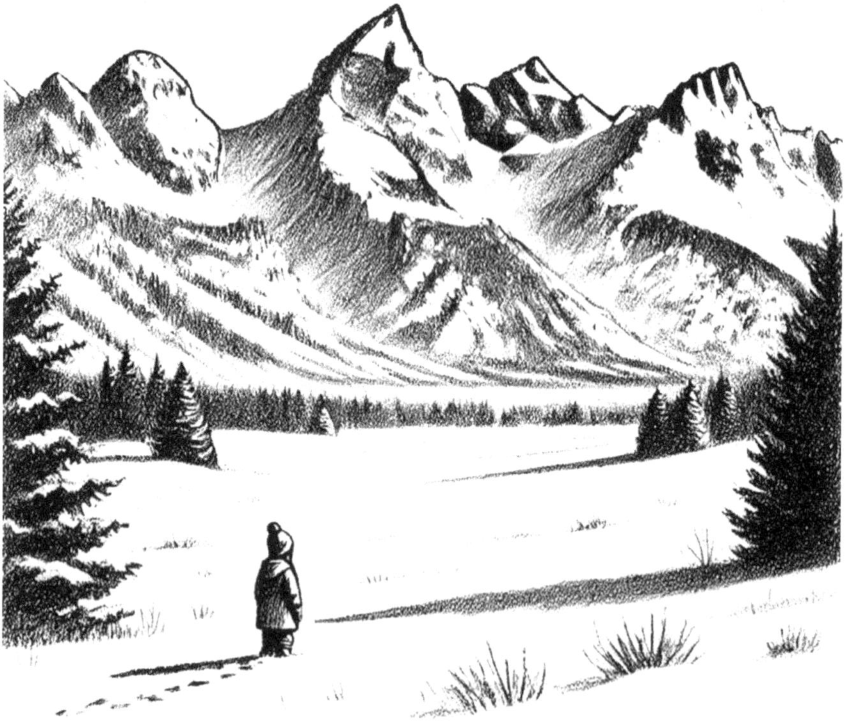

PART THREE
Unfamiliar

CHAPTER TEN
Cold and Lonely

Tatum could feel the bitter chill through all the layers she was wearing. It was an arctic atmosphere that was unlike anything she had ever experienced before and that nothing could have prepared her to encounter. It was the direct opposite of the warmth she felt when the light visited her in the dream earlier that night. More than a persistent coldness, it felt like the complete absence of all heat.

~

Grant had always been what Jill called a "hot body," and it wasn't because of his masculine physique. She was frequently chilly, so she loved snuggling up next to her husband. He was her personal heat-source. Warmth often seemed to be emanating from his body which is why he was happy in shorts, a tee shirt, and flip-flops, even if it was only forty-five degrees outside. Grant, however, had finally met his match. Even under more layers of clothing than he had ever put on, he was almost instantly aware that Kadosh was glacial.

~

The icy air had made its way through every layer of Jill's apparel, pierced the pores of her skin, and seeped into her bones. She checked her surroundings, but nothing looked familiar. How could it? Even if this was the very same spot she had landed in before, everything was now covered in a thick layer of white that wasn't there on either of her previous arrivals in any shape or form. This time it was omnipresent. The ground was white. There were still mountains, but they were blanketed, too. Even though there was snow everywhere, the altostratus clouds that produce snow, which Jill had always considered more of a bluish-gray color, were non-existent. Even the sky was white, like one giant cirrus cloud. The lack of color, quite literally, seemed to have taken over.

Unsure of where to go, but certain that standing in place guaranteed her to not only keep from getting any semblance of body heat going but also go absolutely nowhere, she lifted a boot out of the snow and took a very heavy step forward.

~

Planting it back down again, Kinsey's foot sank about ten or twelve inches into the fresh snow. As he noticed the eerie silence in the still air, he wondered where the other boys were, who was remaining from the small group he had previously left behind at their insistence, and how many new kids had arrived since he had last been in Kadosh.

Finally, his thoughts landed on Trevor in particular. Silently thanking God for another chance to save Trevor's life, he smiled in the hopes that he would be able to find the angry boy again. Then his smile grew bigger, and he let out a small but audible, partial chuckle as he realized how strange it was to be looking forward to seeing someone one who had never been anything but mean to him to such an extreme that he had, at one point, actually tried to kill him. *Forgiveness might even be better for the giver than it is for the receiver,* he thought as it slowly dawned on him for the first time that, at some point, he had forgiven Trevor without even noticing that he had done it. *Forgiveness. Only by the grace of God. Amazing.*

Kinsey continued walking until he realized that his breathing had become heavier. He felt it in his chest, but it was also evident in the steam clouds he made in front of his face with every husky exhale. This was the first of many instances he would wonder about the length of time he had been walking. All he knew at this point was that it hadn't been long. That would eventually change drastically.

~

Tatum slowly began to feel her body warming up from the difficult work of simply walking. What made it so demanding was the fact that she was wading through the deep powder which acted like weights on her feet, and gravity was doing the rest. It reminded her of a lesson at school where they learned about the history of snowshoes.

She couldn't remember all the details, but she was pretty sure they had been invented around five thousand years earlier somewhere in Central Asia. She did remember, however, that they were designed to create a significantly larger footprint for the user, spreading the burden of their body's mass out over a larger area and making the kind of traveling Tatum was doing at that moment a lot easier. *When I find a place to hunker down,* she thought, *I might have to reinvent me a pair of those things.*

~

While the idea of "hunkering down" sounded like a good one to Jill, especially the harder she worked because the increasing fatigue made rest so desirable, it also generated a bit of apprehension in her. She knew that if her body stopped moving without a fire to heat her surroundings, she would eventually freeze to death.

~

For the time being, Kinsey simply decided to keep going. He continued to hope that he would eventually find another boy, Trevor or not, but as minutes turned into hours, and the hours started piling up, Kadosh began to appear as barren as it did white. Each step grew more difficult, and Kinsey felt his body hunching over as his eyes grew increasingly heavy. *So much for track getting me into shape,* he thought. *The team should spend a couple of hours out here. We'd all be as fit as anyone in the district.*

He suddenly had an overwhelming desire for pizza and wondered where that thought had come from. He realized it had probably been the better part of a day since he had consumed any food or beverages. It was the first thought of hunger he could remember since he and his family had woken up from their dreams that told them it was time to go to Kadosh. He wondered exactly how many hours that had been and quickly excused himself for wanting a hot slice of pizza. He didn't even care all that much what was on it. Everything sounded good to him in that moment. Well, not mushrooms, but everything else.

That's when it hit him; fatigue was truly setting in. He was exhausted and needed to find a place to rest before he passed out in the snow.

~

Grant stopped in his tracks and scanned the area for a place to take shelter, both squinting and blinking repeatedly because his eyes wanted to close so badly. *There has to be a cave or something around here somewhere,* he thought as his eyes finally shut. He felt his body grow heavy and his head jerk up as his eyes opened, and he tried to force them wide as he stiffened his body and stood straight up to keep himself from passing out.

Head swiveling, Grant frantically searched the area again for either a sign of life or some kind of shelter. Disappointed at the lack of prospects, he finally decided to keep himself moving and lifted one leg in front of the other in an attempt to both make progress and keep himself awake and alive.

~

Tatum was growing more desperate with each step. It was no longer just her feet but her entire body that felt heavy. Even her arms began to feel as if she was dragging her knuckles through the snow like some kind of arctic Neanderthal. Her thoughts became foggy, her vision started to blur, and the speed of her motions felt like they were gradually reducing, until finally, everything suddenly went black.

CHAPTER ELEVEN
Shelter

Light began to slowly pierce the darkness, and Grant suddenly realized he felt a warmth that surprised him. *Am I still in Kadosh?* he wondered. *Was I even really there, or was it all just a dream?* His eyes fluttered as he tried to open and adjust them. *Why is the light flickering? Where am I? Is that rock?* Grant forced his eyes open and looked around. He was in some sort of a cave, and there was a fire in front of him. Head gently swiveling, he finally spotted people sitting on rocks about ten feet away. Men. Three of them. *Kadosh.*

~

"Trevor?" Kinsey inquired, still trying to focus his eyes.

"Welcome back," Trevor responded. "Unless, of course, you

never left."

"You know I did."

"I know you left camp. How could I possibly know what you've been doing since then?"

"So, you're sayin' nothin's changed," Kinsey mumbled.

"Look around." Trevor stood up and gestured with his right arm. "Everything's changed."

~

Jill nodded in concession as Diane approached her vehemently. "Just like everything went dark a short while after you left the first time, this last one was worse because it got so cold that everything began to freeze. And then the snow came, followed by the winds. It turned into a blizzard, forcing everyone who was still here to scatter like animals, left to find shelter and forage for food on our own."

"You couldn't stay together?" Jill asked, genuinely concerned.

"Are you not hearing me?" Diane shouted. "It was mass confusion. No, we couldn't stay together. We found shelter wherever we could. There's no more camp. No one goes to find new arrivals because it's so dangerous. We know there are people alive out there, probably mostly in caves like we are, but we'll never know for sure how many, and we'll definitely never have the numbers we used to have. You forced us into isolation."

"Sounds like hell," Jill admitted.

"Hell would be better than this. At least we'd be warm."

Huh, walked into that one, Jill thought, keeping it to herself.

"It was bad enough before. You only made things worse."

~

"That's all you've ever done," Trevor stated in the quietest voice he had used since he got into Kinsey's face. Signaling that he had finally finished getting his frustrations off of his chest, he sat back down by the other two boys. Kinsey recognized the red-headed one from before but couldn't remember his name. The other boy, whose hair was a light brown, didn't even look familiar.

"I'm sorry you feel that way," Kinsey finally managed in a tone even quieter than Trevor's final statement. Trevor barely responded by exhaling and waving a dismissive arm. "I mean it," Kinsey continued. "I've only ever wanted to help."

~

"Yeah, well, that didn't exactly work out, did it?" Victor

asked sincerely.

"It did for some," Grant stated matter-of-factly.

Victor looked up and stared directly at Grant who met his gaze. It was the first time Grant had ever seen true sorrow in that pair of eyes, and it filled him with hope that Victor may not be beyond saving.

~

"I wish I'd gone with you," the blonde who Tatum recognized suddenly blurted out. "It couldn't have been any worse than this."

Tatum was stunned as she watched for a reaction from Irisa but none ever came. She didn't try to argue. She certainly didn't agree with the notion either. She simply turned her attention to the ground and sat in silence.

~

Jill hoped that Diane's lack of reaction signaled that she had finally been beaten down so far by this horrible place that she was ready to let go of her stubbornness and try to get home.

~

"Is that why you came back?" the boy Kinsey recognized asked. "To take another group out?"

"Logan," Kinsey blurted out as it finally came to him. "That's your name, right?"

The boy nodded affirmatively.

"The short answer is yes," Kinsey started as Trevor looked up and caught his stare again. "My family has returned, hoping to take everyone with us, but this is the last time."

Trevor looked away again as the brown-haired boy stood up and extended a hand. "I'm Micah."

~

"Nice to meet you, Javier." Grant shook the man's hand.

"Do you really think getting out is possible?" Javier asked.

"My family has done it twice," Grant responded without hesitation.

"I still don't know if I believe that," Victor mumbled.

"It's true," Grant insisted. "I can't make you believe me, but it really is."

"Then I'm in," stated the man Grant recognized from before.

"Brandon," Victor appealed.

"If there's even a small chance of getting out of here,"

Brandon said, turning directly to Victor with an unyielding persistence, "I'm not passing it up this time."

~

"You know as well as I do," Diane pleaded with her friend, "this is impossible. Shayal, don't do this. Don't leave me here."

"I'm not leaving you," Shayal, a tall and slender woman in her forties responded. "I want to go. If you choose to stay here, that's up to you."

~

"It's dangerous out there," Irisa challenged. "More dangerous than ever."

"How so?" Tatum asked before realizing some of the response would be obvious and that she should move the conversation along. "I mean, besides the freezing temperatures."

"Oh, besides that little thing?" Irisa fought back with a heavy layer of sarcasm in her voice. "Well, for one, there's no longer any water to cross."

"What do you mean?"

"It's all frozen over."

"That's great," Tatum insisted.

"No, it's not," Irisa pushed back.

"Shouldn't that make it easier to get to the other islands? Reunite with our families?" Tatum watched as the other girls' heads dropped, and Irisa's confidence in her position increased.

"Tell her, Yanna."

Tatum's eyes shifted from Irisa to the girl she remembered from her last trip to Kadosh.

"Kate and I went looking for food a while back," Yanna started as Tatum's eyes shifted to the girl she had just met for the first time. Kate gave her a nod to let her know she was hearing a true story as Yanna continued. "We ran into a girl named Rebecca who was out doing the same thing we were."

"Why isn't she here with you three now?" Tatum interrupted.

"She refused to come with us," Kate interjected before Yanna went on.

"While we were talking to her, she told us that she and a girl named Natalie had tried to cross the ice to get to their moms. The ice cracked open, and Natalie drowned."

"That's awful," Tatum conceded.

"Yeah," Irisa jumped in to take advantage of the shift in the tone of the conversation, "awful. So, you see, this deep freeze we're all in has made it impossible to escape whether it worked for you before or not. Things aren't like they were out there the last time. We're stuck, and that's that."

"Is that it?" Kinsey asked sincerely. This caught everyone's attention. Every boy stared at him with shocked looks on their faces. "Really. What else?"

"Oh, I don't know," Trevor jumped back in with sarcasm thick as a verbal quilt, "do you remember the part about the blizzards?"

"I do," Kinsey responded immediately.

"I'm not talking about the ones you get at the D.Q. Grill and Chill. There aren't any around. Trust me, I've looked."

"Got it. The point is, I never said this was going to be easy. It wasn't before, and it won't be this time either. But, if we prepare for the worst, we'll have a chance to get out of here and be with our families again. I promise, it's worth it. You said yourself that even hell would be better, so if nothing else, like Logan admitted, it can't be worse than this."

Suddenly, a low thud was heard in the distance, and the ground shook a little. Kinsey's brows quickly furrowed as he tried to figure out what he had just experienced. It happened again. Then again and again. As the thud repeated, it began to get louder, and the size of the ground shakes grew with the noise.

Kinsey looked at Trevor who quickly asked, "Wanna bet?"

CHAPTER TWELVE
Herd and Seen

"What is that?" Kinsey asked, both sincerely perplexed and noticeably trepid.

"Why don't you have yourself a little look?" Trevor responded arrogantly. It was clear that he knew what was causing the commotion, but whether or not he was tricking Kinsey into putting himself in harm's way remained a mystery for the moment.

Kinsey hoped the fact that the other boys didn't protest was a good sign. No one else moved while, slowly, he made his way toward the entrance of the cave, trying to keep his balance. As the ground shaking became almost constant, the sound continued to grow in both quantity and volume. The bright white color came into view, and Kinsey hugged the wall as he kept walking forward.

Finally, the entrance acted as a window. As he got closer, he could see more of the surroundings. Without warning, a massive body passed by the cave, briefly blacking out the view. Kinsey retreated but then couldn't help himself. He inched forward, moving back to where he had just been, and lowered his head to look up and see what the massive creature was.

It was a thirty-foot tall brachiosaurus. Kinsey's eyes widened. He looked on in awe as the long neck got further away. The spinal column was darker in color than the rest of its body but included lighter spots and stripes. It also had a row of small spikes down the middle of its back. He watched as the long, powerful limbs lifted out of the snow and then pounded back down to the ground, both spraying snow and compacting it all in one motion. As the muscular tail ultimately whipped by, Kinsey estimated that it was twice as long as it was high.

He continued to stare as it got further away for a moment before turning his gaze to what was following the enormous creature, and his eyes nearly bulged out of his head. It was another couple dozen just like the first one, and scattered among them were at least twice that number of troodons that looked like raptors covered in feathers. The bird-like animals were about eight-feet in length and had huge eyes. Kinsey continued to silently stare in absolute amazement. In all the time he had spent in Kadosh, he had never witnessed anything like this.

The Four Corners of Winter

~

The pyroraptors didn't stand much taller than Jill's knees, but their length from head to tail was at least eighty percent of her own body length. Not that she was willing to go out there and measure them, or even make herself known to them for that matter. It was a sight to behold, but anything besides observing from a hidden position would have been foolish.

Like the troodons that Kinsey was watching, the pyroraptors were covered in feathers, and their legs were carrying them quickly, creating a spray of snow that reminded Jill of the wake behind a boat. The coloring of those feathers varied with the part of their bodies they were attached to. The top of their heads and the back of their necks were a pale orange color. A thin white stripe separated the orange from jet black which covered the face and front of the neck. The almost overdeveloped forelimbs were a dark, reddish brown and covered curved claws. The hindlimbs were a lighter brown with black feet that included exposed claws, the second of which were enlarged. The rest of the body's plumage was a light grey color and rustled as they ran by.

Jill took a seated position at the mouth of the cave and observed with a smile on her face. This was an opportunity that would never come around again.

~

The group of nanuqsauruses Grant was watching looked like a bunch of furry tyrannosaurus rexes but about half the size. Their fur was a silvery-white that nearly blended them in with the snow, but their much darker fur underneath caused a visual separation. Their movement was slow, but Grant had no doubt that they were ferocious beasts that he was better off leaving alone.

~

Like Kinsey, Tatum was staring at groups of two different dinosaurs. The first was an edmontosaurus, and they were immense. She was ballparking their length at forty feet and their weight somewhere between five and six tons. They were a greenish color with lots of brown spots, bulky hind legs, and shorter, thinner forelegs. Most of them consistently walked on all four of them, but a couple stopped and stood up on their hind legs, causing Tatum to wonder if that was their way of getting a better view and looking up ahead to see where they were going.

Ossified tendons, arranged in a latticework along the neural spines of the vertebrae, started at the top of their necks and ultimately formed a straight line down the back and all the way to the end of their long, flattened tails. Their heads were triangular in shape and ended with something similar to a duck bill.

What a fascinating creature, Tatum thought to herself.

The second group of animals she was watching was made up of pachyrhinosauruses. The greenish skin was similar in color to the edmontosauruses, albeit without the brown spots, and they walked on all fours as well, but that's where the similarities ended. They were large, too, but not as enormous as the first group. Tatum estimated their length at about twenty-five feet and their weight between three and four tons.

They look like lizard-skinned rhinoceroses, Tatum added to her ongoing list of thoughts.

Their skulls bore a large, flattened boss over the nose and another, smaller one over the eyes. The nasal boss also sported a jagged, comb-like extension at the tip and a pommel-like structure at the front. A second comb-like horn rose from the middle of the frill behind the eyes.

God is so creative. It was her final thought before being interrupted by approaching footsteps behind her as Irisa slowly walked over and gingerly sat down next to her.

~

"You were right," Grant stated. "No doubt about it. Kadosh

has changed."

"Yeah it has," Victor agreed.

"Well, now that I think about it, there were dinos here before."

"There were?"

"We ran into three of them on our way out of here. But nothing like this, so you won't be getting any argument from me. Kadosh has definitely changed. A lot, actually. A whole lot."

They sat in silence for a couple of minutes before Victor finally spoke. "I wasn't there the first time you showed up, but the way I understand it is, every time you leave things get worse."

Grant let out a slight chuckle. "I guess that's true."

"Pretty scary, aren't they?" Victor asked as both men continued to stare at the nanuqsauruses.

"Yep," Grant admitted. They sat in silence again, but this time only for about thirty seconds before he added on to his comment. "You know, dinosaurs, Raum, even you aren't going to stop me from doing what I came here for."

"I know that, Grant. I do. I also know I don't want to be here to find out what this place is like after you leave again. I'm still not sure whether or not everything you say is true, but I think I might be ready to find out."

"Good," Grant said, finally looking away from the dinosaurs. Victor did the same and their gazes met. "You're a leader. This will go a lot smoother if we're on the same side."

Victor nodded his head in agreement.

"Now, how do we find the others?"

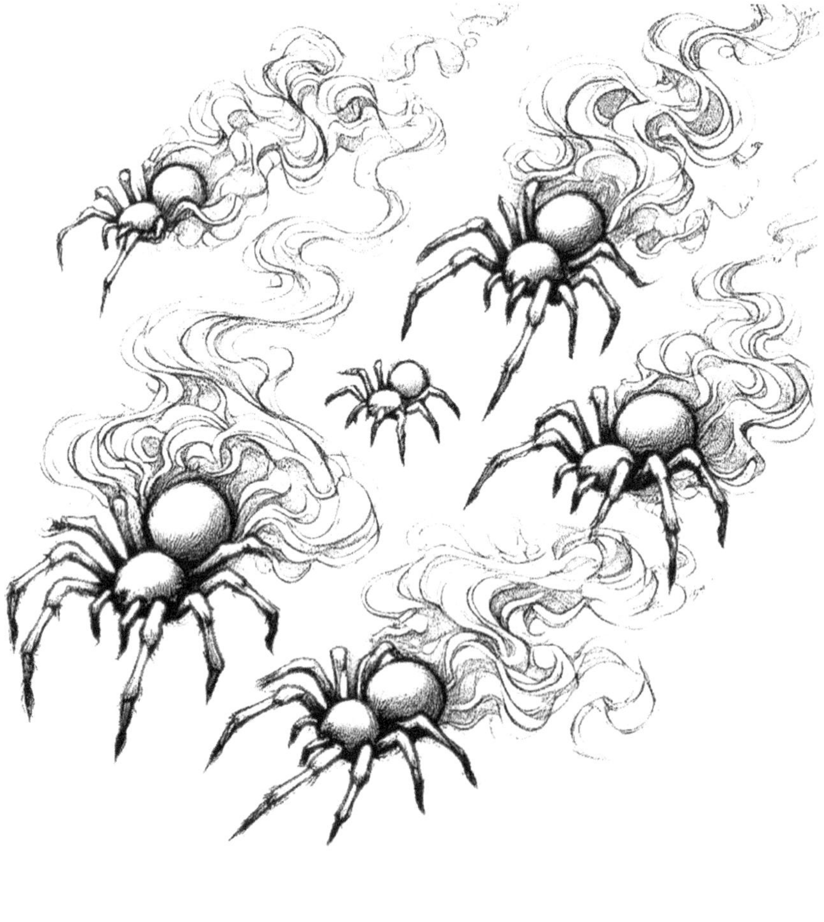

PART FOUR
Searching

CHAPTER THIRTEEN
Wranglers

    The girls were always dressed in their warm clothes they had made from animal hides, but they added extra layers when they left the cave. Tatum had shared some of the clothing she had arrived in, realizing she was much more mobile when she wasn't dressed like the abominable snowman. The girls appreciated wearing items from the "real world," and that fact helped solidify their faith that she had been to Kadosh, made it back home, and returned. However, they also pointed out the possibility that she could have stolen the clothes from other arrivals, even though they didn't really believe that to be true. Overall, the warm clothes turned out to be a morale booster, and in this world, every bit of optimism mustered had a lot of value.

    In the spirit of sharing, Tatum was pleased to realize that, not only had the girls recognized the same need for making snowshoes that she had, but they had also done so with enough volume that they had an extra pair for her. Typically, one of them stayed behind, but occasionally they all went out, and depending on the length of their expected absence, they either added wood to the fire or extinguished it and took torches with them. This time their purpose was to go looking for people, and they weren't sure how long it was going to take because they were hoping that each person they found would lead them to others. So, they decided to treat it like one of their lengthier departures.

Once the layers were on and the fire was out, Tatum followed the other girls toward the mouth of the cave. The cold air hit them all instantaneously, and they quickly started looking forward to returning and getting that fire going again.

They turned right out of the cave, almost one hundred and eighty degrees, and immediately started walking uphill. Tatum realized right away that the extra work was helping heat things up, and she was thankful for it. Still, she hoped their first stop wasn't too far. Not wanting to sound like a child in the backseat of a car on a road trip, she kept that hope to herself and decided to ask a different question. "How often do you guys leave the cave?"

"We rotate who goes and who stays," Irisa started to answer, "but two go out every day. We don't always return with food, but we never come back empty-handed in the firewood department.

Can't survive without it."

~

"You've got that right," added Micah who was sporting one of Kinsey's University of Washington hoodies.

"Yeah, I'm definitely getting that," Kinsey responded with a shiver. "How often do you find food?"

"We don't need to find meat anywhere near as often as the firewood," Trevor stated matter-of-factly. "Depending on the size of the animal, it can last a long time. Look around. We basically live in a freezer."

"Right," Kinsey acknowledged. "Makes sense."

"A lot of the veggies we used to eat won't survive in these temperatures," Trevor continued, "but we have found some wild growing greens that are edible, and even onions."

"Sounds like the makings of a salad," Kinsey blurted out.

Trevor stopped dead in his tracks and threw his head back. "Oh, what I wouldn't give for some ranch dressing."

~

"What I wouldn't give for a hot bath," said Shayal. "I don't even want to talk about how long it's been since I've had one of those."

Jill kept it to herself, but she had noticed an odor back in the cave. She wasn't sure what might be coming from the lack of bathing and what could be from the animal hides the women were wearing. She thought she had her answer now but also knew it didn't matter. They had much bigger things to worry about. She didn't need a reminder of her priorities, but she got one anyway.

Veering off to the left and continuing to climb the hill, Diane was secretly appreciating the thick, pink socks that she had reluctantly accepted from Jill. At first, she had refused altogether, but once she had decided to go on the journey, and after seeing how happy the other women were with their hand-me-downs, she agreed to Jill's offer of socks with the stipulation that it was the outer pair. Diane did not want the ones that had been right next to Jill's feet. That idea disgusted her. She announced they were getting close. "Just a little further this way is where I think we'll find Ella and Claire."

"Sounds good," Jill responded to Diane before reviving the previous conversation. "So, speaking of water, where do you get yours?"

"It's all around us," said Madison, the woman Jill assumed had arrived sometime after the Snyder family last left Kadosh. "We just melt the snow; another reason we have to have a constant supply of firewood."

"Smart," Jill acknowledged, impressed with how these ladies had managed to survive under such extreme conditions.

~

Grant followed Victor, Javier, and Brandon onto flatter ground and into a clearing. Moments later, he spotted another cave and correctly assumed that's where they were headed.

A larger man in both height and weight, Brandon was breathing more heavily than the others and had to stop briefly to put his hands on his knees and try to slow his heart rate down. Everyone took a quiet pause and waited patiently. Grant was the first to speak when he suggested that Brandon try standing up straight and putting his hands on his head to help open his lungs. Brandon took the advice and, although tired and wanting to slump, began to feel better within a few minutes.

~

Approaching the cave, Irisa shouted to make their presence known. "Paris? Zoey? Are you in there?"

"Yep," answered Zoey in a volume that matched Irisa's. "Coming out!"

After the five who knew each other shook hands, Trevor introduced Connor and Ammon to Kinsey. Then Kinsey quietly let Trevor explain, in general terms, the Snyder's previous journeys and the new plan to make one last trip to Raum's island. Kinsey nodded his head in agreement to affirm everything Trevor was saying but, otherwise, let the boys who knew each other do most of the talking.

~

"You really got out of here?" Chris asked Grant, demanding truth just from the tone of his voice.

Grant was a bit taken with how youthful Chris looked to be there among the men and assumed that he must barely be an adult. He was also a handsome and fit-looking young man, causing Grant to hope a little extra that he agreed to make the journey with them since Grant was immediately confident that he had attributes that would be useful along the way.

"I did," Grant insisted. "Twice. And I'm not coming back, so this is a 'now or never' kind of an offer."

"Are you saying it can't be done without you?" Ustav asked with a hint of skepticism.

"I'm not, but there is strength in numbers, and wisdom in going with someone who has already made it out." Wanting to be convincing, Grant decided to reiterate his experience. "Twice."

~

"We've all heard these rumors before, but how do we even know this Raum exists," Claire asked Diane and then turned directly to Jill, "let alone whether or not she saw him, got past him, and made it out of here only to return like some kind of a saint?"

"Who do you think caused the deep freeze?" Jill asked, sincerely perplexed by Claire's naiveté.

"Nature," Ella jumped in with a condescending tone.

~

"Let me guess," Tatum began, "it was like this when you got here.

"Yeah," Paris admitted. "So?"

"So, you've never seen it any other way. You weren't here when it happened."

"Ever heard of an ice age?"

"Those don't happen overnight. Buying that lie just makes it easier for you to believe all of this happened naturally. That you weren't brought here. That your own life didn't open the door for you to *be* brought here."

"You don't know me," Paris seethed.

"You're right," Tatum stated matter-of-factly. "But I do know Kadosh."

~

"He does," Trevor insisted. "I've been here longer than anyone else. I've seen Kinsey come and go twice, just like he said. The world has changed both times. The first time he left, we ended up trapped in darkness. The last time…well, look around. Could that be a coincidence? Sure. But what if it's not?"

The group was silent for what felt like minutes. No one even looked at one another. The weight of what Trevor was saying rode every pair of shoulders within earshot. The battle between fear and doing what one knows is right is something everyone must face in their lives. In this case, for these boys, the battle was happening in their minds and hearts in that moment, and fear was losing. Finally, Trevor decided to give it the death blow.

"We'd be fools not to try."

CHAPTER FOURTEEN
Seeking Unity

The silence continued for a few minutes, but everyone slowly lifted their heads and began to look around at one another. Eventually, they even started nodding in agreement. As the harmony became universal, Grant's eyes locked with Victor's, and they shared a knowing look of gratitude and solidarity. It was a moment that Grant couldn't help being surprised by, and he knew it was because of the work that God had done in between his visits to this bizarre, unrelenting world.

Grant had often heard it said that God is slow. The more he had gotten to know the characteristics and attributes of God since his first trip to Kadosh, the more he disagreed with that premise. He had decided that what people mistook for sluggishness was actually God being patient, and this seemed like a perfect example of that patience paying dividends. He silently thanked the Lord for His timing and both His unfailing goodness and unwavering faithfulness.

As conversation picked back up, the group quickly established a game plan for reaching the others. They would remain in their cave clusters while venturing out in different directions and recruiting everyone they knew how to find. Each new cluster they were able to convince to join their effort would then do the same, stop at nightfall, start again the following morning, and then reconvene at Victor's cave the morning after that one. They agreed that should be enough time to reach everyone they knew was out there, and they hoped they would find a few surprises along the way as well.

At their collective meeting on the third day, they planned to discuss their combined resources, what, if anything, was still needed, and when they would begin the journey to Raum's island. There was a lot to accomplish before then, but they all knew the real hard stuff would happen on the journey itself.

~

It was a long couple of days, and Tatum was having trouble adjusting to her new sleeping conditions, so by the morning of the big meeting, she was just about wiped out. Still, the upcoming events were critical, so she drank some water from her cup made of clay, wished it was coffee, and stretched her arms and legs to try and shake the mental cobwebs out. Rubbing her eyes as she greeted her new roommates in the stark Kadoshian cave, she tried to work through the gravel in her voice and feign an alertness that just wasn't there yet. Truth was, she couldn't be certain it was on its way at all.

It was only about twenty minutes later that girls started showing up for the gathering. Zoey and Paris were first, probably because they lived the closest, but the next pair to arrive was made up of a couple of girls Tatum hadn't met yet, Fiona and Olive. The more people Tatum was introduced to, the more she was struck by the healthy appearance they all had in common. She remembered how malnourished and sickly people were when she arrived in Kadosh the last time because they were having trouble finding food in the dark. So far, the girls seemed a lot more able-bodied now than they did then, which Tatum was surprised by, but also thankful for, because she knew it would be helpful on the excursion they would be starting soon.

~

After the initial greetings were over, Jill followed the women out of the cave as others began to arrive and introduce themselves. Within the hour, close to three dozen women had assembled to join in the discussion. It was quickly determined that, collectively, they had what they needed to begin their journey.

Of course, they would need to find additional food along the way, but they were confident that wouldn't be a problem. Especially when Jill described the attacks by various beasts she had experienced in the past. Rather than going on hunts, they would have to be prepared to defend themselves when they became the hunted. Success generally results in rewards of some kind, but in this case, it would provide nourishment to continue the excursion. Jill smiled at the thought that Raum would unintentionally be helping them in their cause because she knew that fact would really upset him, and she had come to derive pleasure from making him mad. Although his wrath was something to be feared, he was also the enemy, and making the enemy angry felt good in the moment, regardless of what she knew would follow.

The one and only thing stopping the women from starting their expedition the very next day was the fact that not everyone had shown up to the gathering, which presumably meant that not everyone was on board with the quest itself. The response to that realization was every bit as diverse as the group.

"They've obviously made their choice," a beautiful Japanese woman named Hoshi stated ardently. "I say we just go."

"I'm never coming back," Jill stated emphatically but also with a hint of sorrow. "The goal absolutely has to be everyone. And I do mean everyone. If at all possible, I don't want to leave a single person behind, and the One who sent me doesn't either."

"I understand that and agree that the goal should be to include everyone," Hoshi insisted. "I really do. And I sympathize with your concern, but they've been presented with the option, so the truth is that everyone already *has* been included. What else are we supposed to do? We can't force them to come with us."

"No one's going to force anyone," Irisa jumped in.

"Then why wait?" Hoshi asked.

"We just want to give them every opportunity to change their minds and join us," Jill said with sincere compassion.

"We've done what we can," Hoshi fired back. "Some people will never give up their right to make bad decisions, no matter how much time we give them."

~

"Xane's right," Micah insisted as if the answer he was about to deliver was obvious. "If they won't go, then we'll have no choice but to leave them here." He waited for a reaction that wasn't coming as quickly as he had anticipated. "Right?"

Kinsey finally nodded in agreement, unhappy to be

conceding the idea that his original plan to take everyone with him might not turn out to be as plausible as he had hoped it would be.

"We need a deadline then," a short, teenaged boy named Quigley announced. "It's too early to give up on them now, but we also can't wait very long."

"That's fair," Logan agreed. "It may not be ideal, but you have to admit that it is fair."

"How about we wait two full days?" Ammon proposed. "Leave three mornings from now?"

"Sounds like a plan to me," Connor agreed.

"Fine," Kinsey jumped in to agree but also to make a declaration, "but, in the meantime, we do everything we can to convince those who aren't here today that they need to come with us. Their lives literally depend on it, and we have to make sure they fully understand that fact."

Everyone concurred immediately, and the meeting quickly started to break up. Kinsey hurried over to Trevor and quietly exclaimed, "We need to figure out exactly who was missing today and go talk to them right away."

"I agree," Trevor assured him. "Thankfully, I already know who wasn't here, and it's a pretty short list.

CHAPTER FIFTEEN
Smoke

Before she and Jill were to leave on their recruiting mission, Diane wanted to fuel the fire. She could have asked Madison or Shayal to do it since they were staying behind, but the truth was that it was one of the few chores she had in Kadosh that she actually enjoyed. There was a satisfaction she got from, not only keeping the fire going, but also watching it grow when the new wood was added. She also appreciated the crackling sounds it made and the roar caused by the turbulence of the burning vapor, particularly when wind blew into the cave. Of course, the cozy, warm feeling she got from the heat emanating from the flames didn't hurt either.

Diane used a stick to move the existing pieces of wood where she wanted them before strategically placing several new ones on the pile. As they slowly caught fire, she watched the volume and dimension of the blaze increase, felt the warm lick of the flame in the air that gently kissed her skin, and finally allowed a smile to delight her face as she briefly closed her eyes, permitting herself to peacefully marinate in the brief indulgence.

~

"Ready?" Tatum stepped toward Irisa and prematurely interrupted the already short-lived moment of bliss.

Irisa slowly opened her eyes as the smile rapidly faded. "Just about," she responded, gradually standing up. She stuck her hands out, palms open to the flames to feel the heat one more time before a deep exhale. "Alright," she finally stated, already dreading the cold temperatures she was about to endure. "Let's get out there, get this done, get back here, and get to packing."

"That's a lot of getting," Tatum acknowledged.

"There's a lot to *get* done," Irisa immediately responded.

The two girls began to walk out of the cave together but did so in silence after their parting comments. Their minds shifted to the seriousness of the conversation they were about to instigate. Each one was having very different thoughts about it. Tatum was optimistic and anxious to get started, while Irisa wanted it over with because she didn't expect to convince anyone of anything. She agreed that it was something they had to try, but that didn't make her look forward to it at all. Just the opposite. It felt more like an obligation to her, and that just made it a box she had to check so she could move on. She could only assume Paris and Zoey felt the same way. After all, they were the ones that had to go talk to Rebecca, and everyone knew there was no bigger lost cause than the girl who had completely retreated into isolation after witnessing the drowning death of her friend, Natalie.

Those thoughts would have to be put on hold, however, because an interruption came from out of nowhere. They weren't even halfway to the entrance when they were both stopped in their tracks by the sound of a scream coming from behind them.

~

Spinning around toward the sound, Grant and Victor exchanged a quick, perplexed glance at one another before simultaneously starting to run back to the same spot they had just come from. Rounding a curve in the cave wall, the flames swiftly came into view, followed by Javier and Brandon who were both backed up to another wall in the cave with their eyes staring down, fixated on their campfire.

Grant and Victor steadily followed their gaze back to the burning heap of logs, wondering specifically what had their unbroken attention. At first, everything looked completely normal, but after watching it for a moment, they both suddenly noticed something strange about the movement of the smoke coming out at the bottom.

~

Kinsey tilted his head sideways trying to get a better look. Trevor had the same goal but took his effort a step further and lowered himself down on to his haunches. After momentarily wondering whether or not their eyes were playing tricks on them, both boys slowly began to accept the fact that the smoke was not only remaining at ground level instead of rising the way that it normally does, but it was actually crawling out of the fire in bunches that looked and moved like dozens of large spiders.

"What are those?" Trevor finally wondered out loud as he jumped back to his feet and allowed his curiosity to morph into trepidation.

~

"I'm going to go ahead and call them smoke spiders," Jill answered cautiously and with full knowledge that her classification of this new species was right on the nose.

"Is that even a thing?" Shayal asked, with equal parts fear and inquisitiveness combining to make up the tone of her voice.

"Well," Jill began to ponder out loud, "it is when you add the Raum-factor.

"Are you saying you've seen these things before?" Madison asked sincerely.

"Not these exactly," Jill responded as she and Diane, who wiggled her body to amplify her display of feeling grossed out, both watched the smoke spiders start crawling up the walls, "but I have seen stuff like this happen when Raum is trying to send a message."

"Well, he definitely has my attention," Shayal nearly shouted as the fear in her voice overtook the inquisitiveness. "What's the message?"

~

"In my experience," Tatum started, already stating her position emphatically, "he sends things like this because he wants to convince us to give up. Seems like he starts earlier each time I come, too."

The number of spiders continued to increase with every spit of smoke. Kate suddenly shrieked, causing all four girls to back further away from the fire as a significant number of the creatures suddenly turned and began to crawl in different directions toward each of them. The shriek seemed to be contagious as Yanna let out one of her own, and Irisa quickly followed suit.

"What do we do?" Kate yelled in desperation.

~

"I don't know," Kinsey conceded.

"That's not an answer," Micah fretted.

"Well, I don't. I don't know."

"At least try to say something helpful," Micah begged.

Kinsey struggled to come up with anything positive until he suddenly blurted out, "They're just smoke."

"You don't say," Logan mocked.

"What I mean is, I don't think they can hurt you."

"Well, they're still freaking me out," confessed Trevor. "And how do you know they can't hurt us?"

"I don't," admitted Kinsey. "I'm just trying to look at it logically."

"What exactly is logical about smoke turning into spiders?" asked Logan with genuine skepticism.

"Fair point," Kinsey conceded again as he began to back away from the approaching creatures. "Very fair. Call it a guess then. Unfortunately, that's about all I've got right now."

The spiders were blanketing the cave walls all around the men, floor to ceiling, and had crawled right up to each of them in a single-file line as if they were in a stand-off. Briefly, Grant considered the fact that he was surrounded by smoke but didn't seem to be inhaling any. There was no smell and no haze in the air. He wondered if the reason for that was that all of the smoke in the cave was currently being used to generate these strange arachnid-like creatures. Typically, smoke would dissipate in the air, but these things remained as solid as something made of smoke possibly could.

The thought fled as his brain returned to the fact that they were all around him and lined up directly in front of him. He wondered if they would try to do anything and, of course, whether or not his theory about them being harmless was even slightly accurate. The stand-off seemed to last several minutes. Slowly, Grant came to the difficult conclusion that there was only one way to find out. He was going to have to engage them. In that moment, he knew he would either wind up thankful and able to laugh the whole thing off, or he was going to find out he was dead wrong.

CHAPTER SIXTEEN
Poof

Just as Tatum was about to step forward and go on the attack, as if the smoke spiders had the same idea or knew what she was about to do and wanted to beat her to it, they all simultaneously lunged at the girls from every side. They ran up the girls' legs, leapt off walls, and dropped from the ceiling, smothering everyone. When the spiders landed on them, their presence could be felt, but it wasn't because of weight. It seemed more like the movement of air against their clothing or bodies than the mass of something with any substance.

The natural reaction from the girls was to shake and scream, but the spiders wouldn't fall off. They crawled all over them, covering their arms, backs, necks, and hair. It was like a nightmare they couldn't wake up from.

~

Just because the women were older and had more life experience behind them didn't mean they were any less hysterical. The screaming, twirling, and flailing easily rivaled that of the girls. They, too, felt the smoke spiders crawling all over them and even burrowing into their hair and clothes.

No exception, Jill was focused on her hair at that moment and her concentrated gyration included hastily running her fingers throughout her mane to try and get it cleared. It was awful. She could feel the creatures but couldn't see them or what she was doing at all. If she could, she would have been thrilled to watch the effect she was having. When she swept through the strands of hair and connected with the smoke spiders, they swiftly wafted away from her and dissolved into the air.

~

And just because the men had higher levels of testosterone coursing through their bodies, didn't mean they were any less hysterical either. In fact, if his kids could have seen the way he was handling the attack, they probably would have assumed Grant had pounded half a dozen energy drinks and was dancing to an old disco song that only he could hear. They wouldn't even be able to tell whether or not the song was a good one, but knowing Grant the way they did, they would have been confident that, in his mind at least, when it came to disco music, there was no such thing. But even he would admit that these smoke spiders were something far worse.

~

Kinsey was the first to try smacking the spiders running up his arms, and that's when he first saw one vanish. It surprised him so much that he stopped moving for half a second, then came to his senses and started slapping and stomping on every hazy arachnid he could find. "Hit 'em," he yelled. "They disappear!"

The boys hurried to follow Kinsey's direction, and collectively, they were almost instantly smashing the smoke spiders faster than the fire could spit them out. In the middle of it all, Trevor grabbed a huge bear skin blanket from his sleeping area and threw it over the fire, quickly extinguishing it. The flames almost instantly vanished, and the smoke that seeped from the sides continued to act like it was taking the shape of spiders but began to float up in the air like smoke typically did and then dissipated. Everyone breathed big sighs of relief as they realized the horrifying event had ended just as quickly as it had begun.

~

"Phew! I'm glad that's over," Kate announced with several heavy exhales.

"Yeah," Irisa began, "for now anyway."

"Let's try to stay positive," added Yanna.

"Right," Irisa agreed. "Tatum and I are heading out. Why don't you two go ahead and get the fire going again."

"What if they come back?" asked Yanna, clearly afraid.

"Well, we can't really live without fire so…" Irisa purposefully trailed off.

"Can't really live with those things either," Yanna shot back, clearly on the brink of truly freaking out.

"Given the two options," Tatum chimed in, "I'll take the one with the heat source and the harmless smoke bugs over freezing to death."

"I agree," Kate stated with very little conviction.

"Yeah, me too. And what happened to staying positive?" Irisa asked sincerely.

"That was before we started talking about bringing those things right back," Yanna retorted hastily. "I mean, what's positive about a fire that produces excessively aggressive spiders?"

"Okay," Irisa agreed as she looked around the cave for

consensus. "That's fair, right?"

"Yep," Kate confirmed.

"No argument from me," Tatum stated as she threw her hands up in the air.

"There you go." Irisa nodded at Yanna who seemed pacified. "We're going to head out now. Do you want us to wait and see what happens with the fire?"

Yanna shook her head, letting them know it was fine to go.

"We'll be back before dark," Irisa announced as she reached out and touched Tatum's arm to signal that it was time to leave. They immediately began to walk toward the cave entrance as all four of them let out another big sigh.

~

Jill and Diane stepped out of the cave and turned left. Their conversation immediately started with what they had just experienced in the attack from the smoke spiders, how that was a harbinger of things to come, and then slowly shifted to the woman they were on their way to talk to.

Her name was Wanda, and Diane quickly informed Jill that she was going to be a particularly tough nut to crack. She was quite elderly and very set in her ways. Wanda had arrived shortly after the Snyders' previous departure and had chosen to live alone ever since. Diane described her as crotchety, then clarified that she wasn't exactly nasty, but uncompromising in her determination to be left alone. The more Diane talked, the more nervous Jill became about the encounter she was marching toward.

~

Grant's concern over the men he was on his way to meet had increased as well. Victor first told him about Dave, who he described as a nice guy but quiet and under the thumb of the man he lived with, Zeke. Clearly, from the way Victor told it, Zeke was the one that was going to be a problem.

He was, apparently, very strong-willed and displayed an exaggerated masculinity. Grant had always described those kinds of guys as being "full of machismo." Either way, it gave Grant a pretty good idea of what he was walking into. He didn't expect Dave to do much talking any more than he expected a whole lot of listening from Zeke.

~

Less anxious than his parents, Kinsey listened politely as Trevor went on about both Ian and Bryson. He called them troublemakers, which forced Kinsey to stifle a laugh as he thought about the fact that Trevor would have likely described him the same way when they had first met all those years ago. This had him wondering if he would have more in common with these guys than Trevor realized. Unfortunately, Kinsey was underestimating the boys he was about to face, and he would soon find that out in a shocking way.

~

The most terrified of the Snyder family was Tatum. She hadn't started out that way, but as soon as Irisa had referred to Ava as a practicing witch, Tatum's guard had gone up and stayed there. She had never confronted such a thing. Suddenly, she felt like she had been living in something of a bubble because she realized that, without having given it much thought, she didn't even think there were people in the real world who did that. *Isn't that just an evil character in fairy tales,* she wondered to herself. But Tatum could feel it in her soul; she was about to learn first-hand just how real it was.

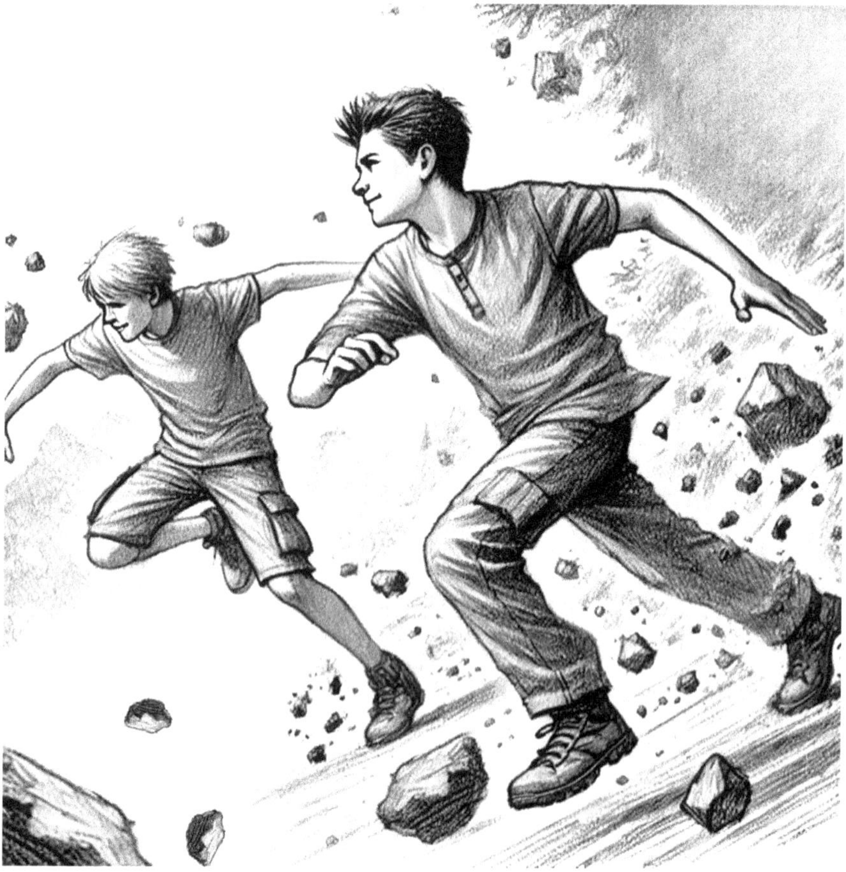

PART FIVE
Polarized

CHAPTER SEVENTEEN
Split

Jill followed Diane up the steep embankment. Both women were experiencing heavier breaths with each stride.

"This is quite the quad workout," Jill admitted.

"Yeah," Diane confirmed. "Feeling it my calves and my butt, too."

"No kidding," Jill agreed as she watched her old enemy, who was now her new friend, reach the top of the hill, step onto level ground, and hunch over to put her hands on her knees and catch her breath. Jill was right behind her and did the exact same thing. "Holy smokes," she said while trying to suck in air. "After that, this next part should be easy."

"I don't know about that," Diane chimed in while raising an arm to point but leaving her head facing her knees. "We'll find out soon enough, though. The cave is right over there."

~

"Okay," Grant conceded as he realized how much he was suddenly craving a glass of water. "Just give me a minute to catch my breath."

"Take all the time you need," Victor said through wheezing that was slightly greater than Grant's.

Grant put his hands behind his head and breathed deeply, visible through his expanding and contracting chest, several times before dropping his arms. "Okay," he finally started, "let's roll."

~

"Ian," Trevor shouted from just outside of the cave's entrance. "Bryson! It's Trevor! Anyone home?"

Kinsey waited patiently about two steps behind and just off to the side of his companion. Suddenly, they both heard a rustling sound and exchanged a brief, expectant look.

"On our way out," a voice interrupted, causing them to look back into the cave.

A few seconds later, a white ball began to emerge from the darkness. At first, Kinsey thought he might be getting another visit from the ball of light he'd seen in his dreams. But, as this one approached, he realized it wasn't made of light, and it wasn't going to stop. At that very moment, it hit him in the forehead and made a splat sound. He quickly recognized the consistency of the leftover mass on his face as snow. Trevor turned to Kinsey with a stupefied look, and before he even knew what was happening, a second snowball pounded his cheek.

~

Jill and Diane hadn't found themselves in the middle of a snowball fight, but their greeting from Wanda wasn't any more friendly. "You ladies better not be here to talk me into this stupid escape plan like those other dummies were trying to do."

After a quick look of befuddlement was exchanged, both Jill and Diane attempted to compose themselves and figure out how to proceed since that was exactly what they were there to do. "Well…"

"Oh, great." Wanda, who looked about a hundred years old but moved more like she was around eighty and had a mind as sharp as a fishing hook, threw her hands up in the air and then used the left one to wave them off. "You're a couple of dummies, too."

~

"Look," Grant started, "I know this isn't an easy decision."

"Easier than you might think," Zeke immediately fired back.

"It's also a really important one," Grant countered.

"This is a last chance kind of a thing," Victor added.

"Yeah?" Zeke was starting to show his persistent anger. "Well, like we already done told the others, decisions already been made. Minds are made up. We ain't goin'. Nothin' you can say to change that. So, you might as well turn around and go. Get yourself started on that suicide mission you got everyone all excited about."

~

"It's not a suicide mission," Kinsey argued. "I've done this twice before, and both times most of us made it out."

"Says you," Ian snapped.

"Yeah, says me. Who else?" Kinsey was letting his frustration show. He didn't want to, but that snowball had gotten things off to a rough start.

"I don't like you," Bryson chimed in.

"You don't even know me."

"I know you showed up and started stirring up trouble."

"Says the guy who introduced himself by throwing a snowball at my face."

"You're the one that came knockin' on our door," Ian shouted, backing Bryson up.

"What door?" Trevor jumped in to do his own backing up. "We all live in caves. Do you really think staying here and accepting this life is all we'll ever have is better than trying to get out?"

"Yeah," Ian began to answer firmly, almost shaking with fury, "we do. So, get a move on or the next snowballs are going to have rocks inside."

~

"Hold on," Tatum pleaded, attempting to diffuse the situation. "Just hear us out."

It was silent for a moment as everyone waited for someone else to say something. Tatum took the opportunity to study Ava. They were about the same age. If there was a difference, Tatum decided Ava could be a year or so younger. Even in a world where everyone couldn't help but become a bit crusty, considering the circumstances, Ava looked extra hardened for her age. There was no warmth, no compassion, and no kindness in her demeanor. Tatum began to feel sorry for her as she considered parts of the Bible, a psalm in particular came to mind, that talked about how God would eventually give people over to their stubborn hearts to walk in their own devices. She couldn't help but wonder if that was what had already happened in Ava's case. Finally, Tatum resolved to give the request for her to join them one last chance and decided to try a different method of persuasion.

"If you don't want to that's fine, but-"

"Well, thank Raum for that," Ava interrupted.

As Tatum was about to jump back in and finish her sentence, Ava's words penetrated her thought process. "Wait. What did you just say?"

"I said, thank Raum."

"Why would you say that?"

"I like it here, and I think I'll like it even better alone."

"Okay, but why are you thanking Raum?"

"He's the god of this world, and I'm staying here to serve at his pleasure."

"There's only one God, and it isn't Raum. And why would you want to serve the demon that brought us here, separated us from our loved ones, and tortured us with these freezing temperatures?"

"That's what you get for disobeying him," Ava admonished Tatum with a snarky glare. "I won't make that mistake."

"Then you'll never know more than this horrible life you know right now," Irisa fought back. "That's a mistake *I* won't make a second time."

After another moment of silence, Ava simply threw her arms up in the air and went back into her cave.

~

Kinsey and Trevor turned around and started walking in silence. Trevor didn't feel the grief that Kinsey did. He expected the meeting to go pretty much the way it had. Kinsey, on the other hand, felt disappointed, defeated, and just plain sorrowful. But he had no regrets. He knew that they had given it every effort and that both Ian and Bryson were going to suffer the consequences of their own decisions.

~

Also walking in silence, Jill and Diane were abruptly surprised to hear Wanda's voice calling after them.

"Diane!"

They spun around in shock.

"What is it?" Diane called back.

"I'll think about it."

"Well, you know when and where. We'll be expecting you."

Wanda gave them a subtle wave and disappeared back into the cave, leaving them with a glimmer of hope.

~

While Zeke had stayed hidden, and they didn't expect to ever see him again, Grant and Victor were experiencing some astonishment of their own as they turned to leave for the second time. Like Wanda, Dave had returned and offered a glimmer of hope that he might join them. The most shocking part of all was that he had shown so much courage in defying Zeke to do so.

~

No one had been completely successful, but at least their parents were headed back to their respective caves with some optimism in their hearts. That simply wasn't the case for either Tatum or Kinsey, and the nail in the coffin, as far as Kinsey was concerned, landed just a few feet away in the form of a rock. He spun around and saw both Ian and Bryson launching more of them into the air. "We're leaving," he screamed.

"Hustle," Ian shouted at the top of his lungs while throwing his third rock.

As if running from gunfire, Kinsey and Trevor began to zig-zag as they sprinted away. In that moment, they knew there was a lot of work to do before they left, but also that the group they already had was the totality of who would be doing it. No one else would be joining them.

CHAPTER EIGHTEEN
The Longest Day; Even Longer Night

Like Victor, Javier, and Brandon, Grant was up at the crack of dawn getting ready for the next day's departure. They were all gathering the things they were going to travel with and building sleds to pull them on. Slowly, men from other caves trickled in with their own cargo, but there hadn't been any sign of Dave. No one had suddenly decided to stay after having committed to go either, so there hadn't been any surprises at all.

There didn't seem to be anyone who was affected by that lack of surprises except for Grant, perhaps because they were all focused on taking the journey to Raum's island for the very first time while Grant had already done it twice. He was about to do it for the third and final time, and his mission was to take everyone he could get to go. Therefore, he couldn't stop looking over his shoulder in the direction of Dave and Zeke's cave and hoping he would finally see his new acquaintance making the decision that the quest was worth the risk before they were gone and it was too late to join them. The more time that passed without Dave's arrival, the more the day seemed to drag.

~

Jill was experiencing an identical lag in time to that of her husband. Days busy with work usually went by quickly, but this one seemed to be moving at a turtle's pace. She knew that Wanda was a cranky old lady, set in her ways, who would likely slow the group down and that most people would probably rather not be bothered by having her along for the journey even though they weren't cruel enough to admit it out loud. But the truth was, Jill didn't want to leave anyone behind, no matter how big of a pain they were, or how much of a burden they would be. The Snyders had arrived in Kadosh with a common goal, and none of them were relenting.

~

Busy cinching up a rudimentary version of a backpack that would hold weapons and tools, Kinsey hadn't managed to let go of the disappointing response he and Trevor had received from

Ian and Bryson. But he wasn't looking over his shoulder because, while he was every bit as steadfast as his parents in their mission, all hope of getting the duo to fall in line had essentially vanished the moment they had sent he and Trevor away amidst a barrage of rocks.

Becoming their targets for stone throwing hadn't left a lot of room for misinterpretation over Ian and Bryson's deficiency of any desire to unite with the group on the following day's expedition. Still, like the rest of his family, his original plan had been to take every single person he could find with him. Although the hope of achieving that was all but gone, and he knew he couldn't try again, the frustration that often accompanies failure continued to nag at him in a way that had become truly annoying.

~

Tatum's thoughts were closer to Kinsey's than her parents', but she was also having trouble getting over how creeped out she was by Ava. She couldn't quite put her finger on it, but she knew in her gut there was something truly wrong with the strange girl. She felt an internal nudge when Irisa had stated that she was a practicing witch. The intensity had increased when she met her, but then it had become truly undeniable when Ava had actually used the phrase, "Thank Raum."

Briefly, she wished she had volunteered for the potentially easier task of trying to convince Rebecca. Both she and Ava seemed like lost causes, but at least Rebecca wasn't a witch. Ultimately, Tatum brushed it off and accepted the fact that it was in God's hands. She and Irisa had been assigned the task of speaking with Ava while Paris and Zoey had made the same attempt with Rebecca. So far, no one seemed terribly optimistic that either of them would be joining the quest, but Tatum couldn't help but hope they would be proven wrong. Ava had been her assignment and so Ava's decision was her primary concern.

She had never met someone who could literally be referred to as a witch before. Nor had she ever met anyone she feared could be so heavily under the influence of demons. *There's nothing more I can do,* she began to silently pray, *but you can, Lord. You can do anything. You promise never to leave us or forsake us. That includes Ava. I won't give up on her because I know you haven't either.*

~

Nightfall came but almost no one could sleep. Not the Snyders, not the people who were joining them on the terrifying adventure that would start the following morning, and not the holdouts. In fact, no one in Kadosh was sleeping. Raum and both everyone and everything under his command were awake and aware that another war was brewing.

~

Grant's eyes were drawn to the licking flames of the fire about five or six feet away. It was a clear reminder of the cold times that were ahead. But he was far more concerned about the fact that he had seen no sign of Dave, and time was swiftly running out.

~

Jill was turned away from the fire, staring into darkness and hoping that it would make her tired enough to fall asleep. The truth was, however, that she was plenty tired. Still, her mind wouldn't pause the thought process long enough to allow the sleep she so desperately needed. It was far too busy concerning itself with both Wanda's decision and the days that lay ahead for everyone who would choose to go. She knew better than anyone, after all, just how full of danger those days would be.

~

Kinsey had prayed a lot that day, and he found himself lying on the cave floor continuing to do exactly that. He knew they had done what they could to get ready for the journey that would start in mere hours. He also knew there were things they would soon face that they couldn't possibly prepare for. Prayer was not only the greatest weapon he had, but it was also all he had left that he could do for Ian, Bryson, himself, and everyone who would be looking at him to get them home.

~

Unlike the rest of the girls trapped in Kadosh, Ava had fallen sound asleep. In fact, although she didn't know it, and there were no other girls around to hear it, her snoring echoed off the cave walls. But there was One who heard her snoring, and He gently entered her dream.

Ava found herself surrounded by darkness. There wasn't even the most obscure hint of light anywhere her eyes could see. She didn't dare move because she didn't know where to go. Was it safe to take even a single step? For all she knew, she was perched at the edge of a cliff. There was no way to tell without risking a fall. She cradled her own body then slowly let go and began to reach into the darkness but didn't sense anything. It was a terrifying feeling. She was trapped, alone, and unable to sense anything but herself.

She didn't even realize she was crying until a dampness emerged just below her right eye and then streamed down her cheek. Suddenly, she realized her body had begun to quiver. It wasn't because of the cold; she was used to that. It was fear. Fear had overtaken her, and there was nothing she could do to stop it.

"It doesn't have to be this way," came a gentle whisper, breaking into the silence and penetrating her perceived isolation.

"What?" Ava practically shouted through fiercely gnashing teeth. "Who's there?"

"I am the Word." The Voice spoke with authority, and suddenly, as if someone had flipped a switch, everything lit up so brightly that Ava immediately had to close her eyes and shield her face from the intensity. "I am the bread of life," the Voice continued, and with it came a welcome warmness.

Without her even being aware of it, Ava's teeth stopped gnashing, and her body stopped quivering. Her fear was instantly replaced with a sense of comfort she had never known before.

"I am." The Voice concluded the declarations with the simplest of them all.

Ava could suddenly discern who this was. She slowly gained confidence and began to open her eyes. "You're the One Tatum mentioned." She spoke softly as, out of the light, she saw a human hand extend toward her. The arm was draped in a white robe, revealed a deep scar, and was surrounded by the blinding light. In fact, Ava abruptly recognized that He was the light. "You know who I am, don't you?" she asked.

"I do."

"You know what I've done and who I have served."

"I do."

"How can you even look at me?"

"I made you to be with me, and I will forgive you if you ask me to."

"Why?"

"Grace."

"I don't deserve it."

"Grace is getting what you don't deserve. Mercy is not getting what you do deserve. I offer both. In this dream, you have felt what it is like to do things your way and end up alone. I'm showing you what it's like to live with Me and fulfill the purpose you were created for. Now, will you take my hand?

CHAPTER NINETEEN
The Door Closes

Kinsey was sitting at the mouth of the cave waiting for the sun to pierce the darkness. It had been a long, sleepless night. The lack of rest was troubling considering the journey that laid almost immediately in front of him. Having done something similar twice before, he knew what to expect, and what he expected was both emotional and physical exhaustion. Kinsey was confident that starting off already fatigued was going to set him up for a quick burnout, and he was trying to ponder ways to combat that but was distracted by the same things that had kept him awake to begin with.

Of course, a chunk of the concern was surrounding the quest he and the others were about to embark on. But the largest part of his worry was concentrated on those who might miss the opportunity altogether. Still, at the forefront of those thoughts was the frustration he felt over the reaction he and Trevor had received from Ian and Bryson. While he knew it was their decision to make, he couldn't help but wish and pray that the Lord would pester them into making the right one before it was too late, and that deadline was fast approaching.

~

Just as the long-awaited light finally began to peek into the darkness, Diane sat quietly next to Jill. "Ready?" she whispered.

"For the most part," Jill quietly answered.

"What part isn't ready?"

"The part that wants everyone to join us," she admitted. "No matter how unrealistic that is."

"I get it. What's that expression though? 'Let go and let God' or something like that?"

"That's it," Jill confirmed. "It's the 'let go' part I struggle with." Jill thought for a moment and then turned to look at Diane with a confused expression on her face. "When did you start quoting Christianese?"

"I'm not entirely naïve to the concept of Judeo-Christian values and lifestyle."

"Again, since when?"

"Since forever. Familiarity with and acceptance of something aren't necessarily the same thing, though."

"True," Jill agreed. "Well, whatever changed your mind, I like you a lot better this time around."

Diane let out a little chuckle before responding. "Yeah, sorry about that. I was pretty angry before. Still doing my own bit of letting go, I suppose. Anger can be an addiction, and recovery is a process. I think this pseudo-Ice Age was my rock bottom."

Jill nodded in agreement and stared at the increasing glow of the rising sun. "Well, whatever it took, I'm glad you're finally ready to do this."

"I don't know about ready," Diane responded. "Willing, yes, but ready? I guess we're going to find out."

~

As the sun completed its daily duty of pushing the darkness out of the atmosphere, those who managed to catch a bit of elusive shuteye began to rouse. Just moments later, Grant noticed men approaching from several directions, and he began to accept that they would be leaving within the hour. It was becoming increasingly unlikely that Dave would be joining them. "Guess it's about that time," Grant mentioned to Victor.

"Guess so," he agreed.

~

Everyone who was expected to go on the journey arrived within about forty minutes of one another. Tatum was relieved to see that no one had changed their mind and decided to stay. Unfortunately, there had also been no shocking appearances from people who had said they weren't going either. The time had finally arrived to accept the group as it was and begin the quest to Raum's island that she and her family had returned to Kadosh to embark on.

~

So, the boys did exactly that. They were dressed in a combination of the clothes they had arrived in Kadosh wearing, what they were able to fabricate out of animals they had hunted and killed, and for some of them, what Kinsey had been willing to share after he realized he had overdressed despite the weather that he correctly assumed would be similar to the Arctic tundra. Many of them were also sporting makeshift backpacks or pulling sleds full of supplies as they headed away from the cave, traveling the same path that Kinsey had previously watched the herd of massive brachiosauruses and the much smaller troodons take just a few, however long, days earlier.

The sleds and the shuffling feet from all the boys walking were making a rhythmic "fluff and crunch" sound with the snow, and the deepening breaths were creating small rising clouds in front of each of their faces as they trudged on, distancing themselves from the caves that had been temporary homes for them. The mood was somber, and the thoughts were mixed with fear, wonder, and anxiety, but at that moment they were all silent.

Suddenly, a distant voice broke through the sounds of crunching snow, causing the boys in front of Kinsey to turn and look behind them. A little late to the party, Kinsey hadn't heard the voice but turned to see what the other boys were looking at. His eyes widened as he saw Bryson running toward them, desperately shouting to get their attention with such vigor that he tripped and tumbled down the hill by their cave. He somersaulted on the ground, flipping so many times that Kinsey wondered if the saying about a rolling stone gathering no moss was the opposite in a winter wonderland, and whether or not it actually increased in size like when someone builds a snowman.

~

Grant began to smile as he watched Dave disappear into a pile of powdery snow and then pop back up like a jack-in-the-box. Everyone around him began to chuckle, and the laughter became contagious. It was a welcome sound, and an even more welcome sight, as Dave got back to his feet and started approaching with a bit more caution once he realized he had their attention, and they were no longer going to leave without him.

~

Laughter turned into clapping and cheering as the women offered a loud hurrah to Wanda who tried to brush the whole thing off both physically with the waving of her arms, and verbally with her snide commentary. "Are you the welcoming committee or the peanut gallery? Either way, that's enough. Let's just get this show on the road."

~

Tatum could hardly believe her eyes. Not only was Ava approaching, which seemed like an impossibility until that exact moment, but she looked like a transformation had taken place in the short time since she had seen her. Tatum remembered thinking about the fact that she looked unusually cold and hard for her age. Even for this place. While it was obviously the same girl, her entire demeanor had definitely changed. It was warmer and softer, like light had somehow pushed the darkness out the same way the sun had at dawn just a couple of hours earlier.

As a tear rolled down Tatum's cheek, Ava walked straight up to her, and Tatum found herself lunging forward at Ava and giving her a big hug. As if Tatum hadn't already been surprised enough in that moment, Ava hugged her back, gripping her tightly, and began to weep with abandon.

The rest of the girls looked on in shock. They had never seen anything to indicate this side of Ava existed.

Finally, Ava pulled away, wiped her tears, and stared at Tatum as she sniffled. "I told Him I didn't want to do things my way anymore; I wanted to be with Him. He told me to go with you and everything else would fall into place."

Tatum smiled back at her knowingly. "Then let's get going."

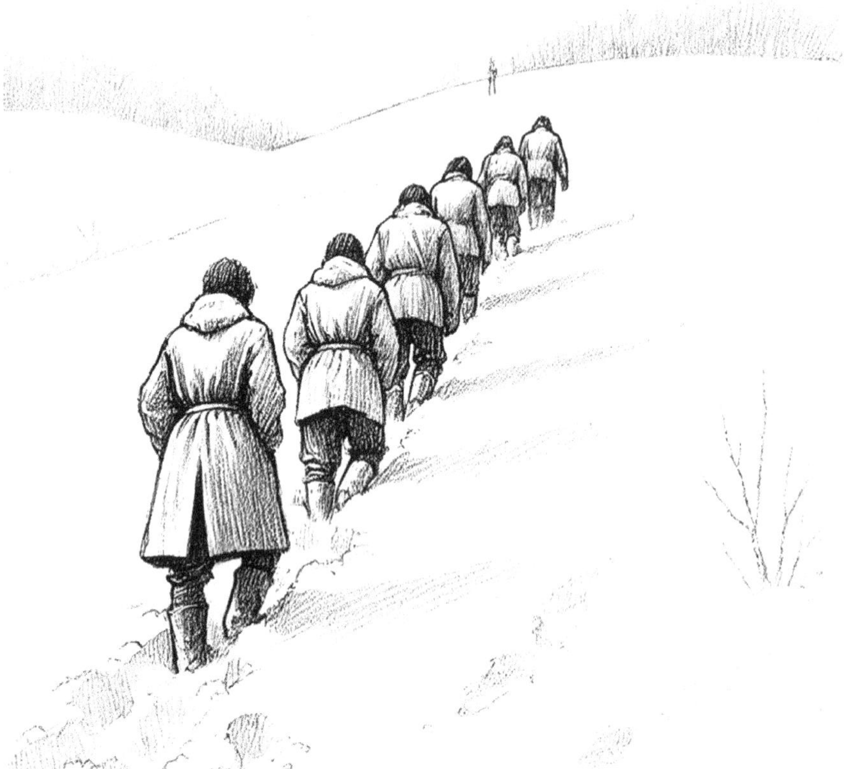

PART SIX
The Final Quest Begins

CHAPTER TWENTY
White on White

Although the continued rhythmic "fluff and crunch" sound from the shuffling feet of the men walking in the snow, combined with the gliding of the sleds to make a unique soundtrack on their journey, it was otherwise very quiet. Everyone was deep in thought and working hard to carry their loads, so the speaking was at a minimum. Thankfully, the demanding nature of the arduous trek they were on was increasing blood flow and keeping their bodies warmer than they otherwise would have been. Still, there wasn't one among them that would have argued that the conditions were anything but glacial.

In addition to the silent men crossing the vast, frosty terrain, the environment itself seemed eerily uncommunicative. Other than a few birds that soared high above them, wings flapping but hushed by the distance, nothing from the animal kingdom had even been seen since their departure. The deep thoughts ruminating in Grant's mind at that moment were centered on the fact that he knew well, while Kadosh might be quiet, Raum was still watching.

~

All four of the Snyders knew that it was true, including Jill, who was right then facing miserable conditions as she and the other women fought a strong headwind that added a howl to their musical experience. They had only been walking for a few hours, but frequent gusts were fighting the heat their exertion was generating, and the constant battle was intensifying the cold temperature, making the entire situation nearly unbearable.

No one had said it out loud yet, perhaps because they wouldn't be able to hear one another, but they were all wondering when it would be time to take a break and build a fire in a cave somewhere so they could warm up and get some rest. However, they also knew that they needed to push forward, both because they had a long way to go and because they needed to save their breaks, knowing that things would likely get even worse.

~

The Four Corners of Winter

Tatum found herself wishing she had been shrewd enough to bring some protective eyewear. She would have preferred some ski goggles, but at the very least even a regular pair of cheap sunglasses would have helped block the wind, and increased visibility would have very much been appreciated. She was confident that the rest of the girls would be grateful for them, too. Even if she had only brought one pair, she would have been willing to share to give everyone a break. Whoever had them on could take the front and lead the way. *If only,* she thought to herself, a little saddened by the fact that such a mundane wish could be considered the height of her fantasy in that circumstance.

~

Leading the way, Trevor suddenly stopped in his tracks. The other boys were all behind him and slowly fanned out to create a single-file line on both sides of him. Everyone squinted their eyes and pointed, wondering at first if those very eyes were playing tricks on them. Quickly, they determined that they were indeed staring at an arctic fox with a dark bluish-gray coat that made it pop off of the white snow. It was between two and two and a half feet in length.

Unfortunately, as it bared its teeth and growled like a warning against taking any additional steps toward it, further examination of the scene revealed that the threat didn't end there. It was actually traveling in a large pack, the extent of which no one could be sure of because the rest of them were all white and camouflaged by their frigid surroundings.

~

They were in the middle of a standoff. No one was moving. Grant could hardly believe what his visual sense was insisting was right in front of him. It would be easy to assume that the nanuqsauruses would have been the most surprising thing he had seen since his third arrival in Kadosh, but he had the security of the cave then. At this moment, he couldn't imagine being more vulnerable.

Therefore, what looked like at least three polar bears, was giving him an even bigger shock than the nanuqsauruses had. He silently guessed they had to be a good eight feet long and weighed a bare minimum of eighteen hundred pounds apiece. To make the scene even more alarming, they were staring the group down from no more than fifty feet away.

~

The women were staring at animals that looked more like what the boys were facing than what the men were right that second. They could see at least half a dozen arctic wolves which were more than twice the size of the foxes and plenty menacing.

~

Unlike most of the ferocious animals everyone else was confronted with, the ones less than forty feet away from Tatum and the girls were covered in thick, dark, oily fur that made the entire group stand out in stark contrast to their snowy surroundings.

At about seventy pounds, the wolverines were a little bigger than the average dog, but they were all muscle and very intimidating. It was at that extremely inopportune point that Tatum realized she had to pee. While it would be very difficult to be successful, she knew she had no choice but to hold it until she and the girls had, hopefully, survived the encounter.

~

Unfortunately, that hope seemed slightly elusive to Grant as he and the others all stared at the bears in front of them that easily weighed as much as any ten of them combined. Just as Grant was wondering how long the staring contest was going to last, the carnivorous creature in the middle stood on its hind legs and roared ferociously.

"Oh, crap," was all Grant could say out loud, although no one could hear him. The sound caused him to remember Kinsey's story about the Kodiak bear he and the other boys faced during the Snyder's first trip to Kadosh and made him think this was something akin to a battle cry.

~

The women all unconsciously stepped backward just a few inches as the wolves simultaneously lowered their heads toward their paws and looked like they were about to pounce. The growling had intensified, and their teeth were all visible, acting like a warning that the women wished they could adhere to. Had they been close enough, they would have been able to see the slobber dripping off the sharp canine teeth and hitting the snow shortly before transforming into an icy substance.

~

Without any warning, the foxes formed a single-file line and began to circle the boys, making it clearer that they were dealing with a number somewhere in the vicinity of three dozen. Slowly, the boys began to draw out their weapons.

~

The wolverines had become erratic, kicking up snow all over the place and making guttural, throaty, growling sounds that caused trepidation amongst the girls. Panic began to set in as they realized they were about to do battle with a bunch of wild animals who were under the command of Raum and would not be satisfied until each and every one of them was dead.

CHAPTER TWENTY-ONE
Seeing Red

"Don't move unless they do," Grant commanded in a loud stage whisper as the bear in the middle continued to stand on his hind legs and roar with great intensity. The other two flanked him and were both quiet and still, remaining on all fours.

"How long do we wait?" Chris asked.

"As long as it takes."

"As long as it takes to what, exactly?"

"As long as it takes to get out of this alive."

~

"It's good to have goals," Madison stated with a hint of dry sarcasm without taking her eyes off the ravenous wolves.

"And, if you're going to have them," Claire chimed in, "that's a good one to start with."

~

Weapons now at the ready, the boys were completely surrounded by the foxes who continued to move in a circle. The chorus of yelps was growing in both force and volume, practically terrorizing the silent boys who had bunched up in the circle with their backs to one another and facing their tormentors ready to defend themselves.

"What are they doing?" Bryson asked no one in particular.

"You ever heard the phrase 'cunning as a fox?'" Ammon responded.

"I think so," Bryson answered him. "Or, at least, something like it."

"This is the smartest predator out here."

"How does that answer my question?"

"So, we might not know what they're doing, but they do. And we should be very afraid."

~

Suddenly, one of the wolverines lunged at Fiona with its claws out and ready to slice. Thankfully, she had a stick in her hands and instinctively turned her hips away from the animal, pulled the stick back, and then swung forward. She clubbed the wolverine in the head like one would only expect from a Major League Baseball designated hitter. Unfortunately, there was no time to cheer. Immediately, the other wolverines began to attack the group.

~

"They moved," Chris shouted as his eyes shifted from the massive bear who was shaking his head like a slapstick cartoon character who had just been walloped with a mallet to the two that were charging toward the men.

Brandon took a claw swipe to his left arm as he jammed a spear into the left shoulder of one of the bears. Immediately, red blood began to seep out into the white fur.

~

Hoshi kicked a wolf in the side of the face and then quickly pulled back on her bow and released an arrow. It was a direct hit, puncturing the side of another wolf that was leaping toward Ella who had her back turned and never knew how close she had come to being the victim of a voracious chomp. The wolf landed with a whimper and then laid quiet.

Nearby, Jill surprised herself by swinging a stick like it was a golf club and uppercutting a charging wolf in the jaw. At the sound of another whimper, Jill's eyes went wide. She was sure she broke the bone and couldn't help but feel bad for the animal, but she valued her own life and the lives of the women around her more highly, making the guilt dissipate quickly.

~

Connor felt the weight of the fox landing on his back and immediately began to spin, first to his left, then his right, repeating the motion over and over again while also trying to grab at the snout of the animal that was gnashing at him.

Finally, Connor's left hand clutched the fox's muzzle tightly. It was a pleasant surprise to the fearful boy, but he hung on and continued to squeeze, increasing the intensity of his grip. Stretching his right arm across his chest, he reached back and took hold with both hands, using his grasp on the animal's nose and jaw to peel him off his back and bring him around in front of him.

Letting go with his right hand, he leaned back and retracted his arm to gain some momentum, then swung it forward, punched the fox in the gut, and released him. As it lost breath and its body fell toward the ground, the next thing it felt wasn't the snow but Connor's foot in his side as he got punted about six feet away from the boy he had attacked from behind.

~

Zoey and Paris were back-to-back, fighting as a team, and both hit their marks at the same time, however, with different results. Zoey released her bow, and the arrow penetrated the wolverine's chest, dropping it instantly. Paris' arrow struck her wolverine in the side, causing it to collapse but then jump right back up and dance around like it was trying to get away from both the pain of the wound and the weapon that had caused it.

~

The polar bear struck Victor in the right arm with so much force that it knocked him off his feet. He landed hard enough to disappear in the snow and didn't get up right away.

Javier abruptly stepped in front of his friend and threw his spear at the bear who quickly knocked it away like he was batting a mosquito. As if that weren't intimidating enough, he then snarled and growled louder than the men had ever heard before. He followed it up by staring down at Javier as if lunch was about to be served. Javier didn't need to see a menu. He knew he was the main course.

To his surprise, however, another spear suddenly burst through the bear's chest, causing him to look down at it, then back up to Javier, before falling face-first into the snow with his head nearly landing between Javier's feet. Shocked, he watched the animal impact the snow then looked back up to where the bear had once been standing. In his place was his new friend Grant whose hands were still in the position they had been when he had plunged the spear into the bear's back. Javier breathed a sigh of relief and swallowed his anxiety as Grant finally released his hands and dropped his arms to his sides.

~

Jill stood above the wolf and pulled the spear back out of it. She watched the white snow turn red as she tried to catch her breath. She looked around at the carcasses littering the ground. All belonged to wolves. Not a single woman was dead. *Raum must be so disappointed,* she thought as a grin began to creep up toward her nose.

~

Kinsey watched as the last of the foxes ran off in retreat. He scanned the group. There were some injuries, but everyone was alive. He briefly wondered what Raum would send next but quickly put the thought out of his mind. It was pointless. There was no way thinking about it could prepare them. This was a moment for enjoying the success of winning their first battle, and that's exactly what he was about to tell the group.

~

"Let's find shelter and build some fires," Tatum announced. "We need to treat the wounded, get some rest, and prepare ourselves to go again at dawn tomorrow. In the meantime, we should thank God for using Raum to send us dinner. Let's gather our meat.

CHAPTER TWENTY-TWO
Partaking

The search for a cave that was large enough to give everyone shelter for the night took more than an hour and proved somewhat unsuccessful in that the men had to split up into two separate areas, although they weren't far apart. Regardless, their post-win enthusiasm never waned even though they had to haul a bear around with them that they estimated could weigh as much as two thousand pounds. In fact, by the time they built fires and began to carve meat out of it, they were so exhausted it may as well have weighed ten thousand pounds.

Grant wished he had some salt, pepper, garlic, and maybe even a little bit of thyme to add to his meat but was otherwise very pleased with his dinner. In fact, he was delighted to be having dinner at all. He couldn't help but wonder if the rest of his family had food to eat that evening.

~

Jill's line of thinking was similar to that of her husband's. She was wishing she could add salt, pepper, garlic, and, in her case, a bit of rosemary, and possibly some kind of berry to her wolf meat. However, also like Grant, she was thrilled just to be eating and knew that what she was shoveling in her mouth could easily be a whole lot worse. While she was focused on her food and missed her family, too, Jill also looked up from her meat and glanced around the room, determining to start getting to know the women she was traveling with.

"Remind me where you're from, Shayal."

"Denton, Texas," she answered right away. "Right between Dallas and Fort Worth but about forty-five minutes to an hour north of those."

"I've never been there, but I've heard of it," Jill responded. "What do you do there?"

"We own a hotel, so that's where I work."

"Who's we? You married?"

Shayal nodded affirmatively. "I am married. His name is Marut."

"Is it just you and your husband?"

Shayal nodded again. "We wanted kids. That was the plan. It didn't work out though."

"I'm sorry," Jill responded with a sincere sadness entrenched in the tone of her voice.

"Instead, we both worked and lived at the hotel, watching the happy families come and go. I got bitter, and we ended up here."

"Now you're going home," Jill reassured her, "and you can do better."

Shayal thanked her with a smile. She was beginning to feel hope for the first time in a long while.

~

Tatum took another bite of wolverine meat and suddenly realized that she had not felt satiated since she and her family had left home. It was a good feeling and one shared by many others which became obvious as she looked around and noticed that people were beginning to relax. It reminded her of her relatives watching football after the big Thanksgiving meal.

She anxiously anticipated getting back home and smiled as she thought about her brother saying that this was the last trip the family would be taking to Kadosh. As grateful as she was for their Kadoshian experience, Tatum was ready to move on with her life and feel a semblance of normalcy. Of course, she couldn't even pinpoint what that was, what it would be like, or even if she'd be able to recognize it when it happened.

Confident that she would never forget Kadosh or even be able to completely let go of the experience, she was also certain that these life interruptions that included major adventures during what only turned out to be a blip back home were not included in whatever normal turned out to be. All she really knew was that it had been missing for a long time, and she had been quietly hoping that heading off to college would be the break she needed to find it. Of course, she had to get out of Kadosh first.

~

What Kinsey hoped would be a good night of sleep was all that separated him from that moment and the next leg of the adventure. He had felt a sense of urgency each time he'd been to Kadosh, but there was something different happening this instance that he couldn't quite put his finger on. It was like an instinct he had, telling him that, while the first trip changed things for his family, this was the one that was going to change things on the grandest scale.

He was exhausted. He'd barely slept the night before, and this had been a day full of physical exertion. Particularly the way it had ended. Still, he was so anxious that he didn't feel like lying down and going to sleep. But the rest of the group was unwinding and definitely heading in that direction. He hoped desperately that he would get there soon, too.

~

Grant was out like a light and dreaming heavily. He had been called by the University of Washington Husky basketball program's head coach and informed that he had a year of eligibility left. They wanted him to play.

Panic set in as it quickly devolved into an anxiety dream. *I should be excited about the opportunity,* he told himself, confused by his own self-doubts. *I'm too out-of-shape. I don't have the hops I used to have. I don't have the same endurance either. I can't keep up. Who am I kidding? I probably won't even be able to fit into those shorts. I'll be a laughingstock.*

Grant jerked himself awake, but it took a minute or so for him to realize it had been a dream. He looked around, having temporarily forgotten where he was. Finally, reality set in. *Kadosh. Ugh. This isn't any better.*

~

Jill was awake, too. But it wasn't a dream that had awakened her, it was the hard ground she was supposed to be sleeping on.

After turning over and trying to find a comfortable position for what seemed like the four hundredth time, she had nearly given up. She missed her bed like never before. She missed her pillow just as much. And she even missed her husband's snoring. Jill couldn't help it; she giggled to herself when she recalled the argument before the first trip to Kadosh when she had insisted that she didn't snore, and Grant had informed her that she not only snored but sounded like Chewbacca when she got going.

Thankful that Kadosh had helped them rekindle the fire of their relationship, all she could do in that moment was hope that Grant missed her Wookie sounds the same way she missed his.

~

Tatum's eyes fluttered. She wasn't fighting sleep; she just didn't believe it was coming back until it finally did. Exhaustion truly took over, and she slipped into unconsciousness. It wouldn't be until she woke up again that she would know to be thankful for that extra couple of hours of sleep. Rest would prove even more elusive as the expedition continued.

~

Kinsey's eyes fluttered, too. But, in his case, he was waking to a beam of light poking into the cave. As he regained consciousness, a grin began to form on his face. It wasn't that he didn't have concerns about what was ahead for him and his fellow journeymen. That would be foolish. But he was anticipating the good parts of what he had come to expect on the experience he was now on for the third time.

Comradery. That was one of the good things.

Reunion. That was another.

The warmth of the light. That was his favorite. It was the love of God, and nothing could top it.

Home. That was a close second and the final step. It was a long way off at this point, but it wouldn't get any closer unless they got up and got going. Another big day was beginning, and there was no telling what that day would bring.

CHAPTER TWENTY-THREE
Forging Ahead . . . While Possible

As Tatum stepped out of the cave, she was shocked by the beautiful sight in front of her. The sun was shining brightly, illuminating everything below it including the very thing that had Tatum's full attention. It was as though a field of gorgeous ice flowers had bloomed on top of the snow overnight.

The Snyders had spent a day at the Woodland Park Zoo a couple of years earlier, and there was a two and a half acre rose garden just outside of it that was open to the public free of charge. It had more than three thousand roses from over two hundred types and was one of the most beautiful places Tatum had ever been, but it paled in comparison to what she now had in front of her.

She could barely believe her own eyes. It was easily one of the most amazing things she had ever seen, and she briefly wondered if a team of ice-sculpting elves had crawled out of the trees and worked all night to create such a magnificent winter wonderland for the girls to wake up to. Tatum could only stare in silence at the pure magnificence of it all.

Suddenly, her mind drifted back to the divi-divi tree on the beach that she and the other girls had seen from their raft on her second trip to Kadosh. That's when it hit her. She knew in an instant that this was a message of encouragement from the One who had called the Snyder family to return. He was letting everyone know that He was watching their excursion and that He had their backs.

The realization gave her a deep sense of both hope and gratitude. In a place of extreme cold, ice flowers suddenly filled Tatum with warmth from the inside out. She couldn't wait to gather the troops, show them the message, and then press on toward Raum's island.

~

The adrenaline rush from the victory over the bears had mostly worn off while they slept, but the encouragement that came with the field of ice flowers that had "bloomed" overnight had recaptured a significant amount of enthusiasm for most of the men. Of course, there were a few who brushed the event off as a weird coincidence, but they couldn't explain it and had to admit that they'd never seen anything like it.

Either way, the general feeling of inspiration amongst the group was at its highest peak since Grant's arrival, and their determination to get to Raum's island had never been greater. After some leftover meat, the men packed their things back up and moved on for the day, ready to make as much progress as they could before another night of rest.

As the skies began to slowly grow dark, the positive attitudes stayed strong. Conversation was jovial, and they were moving along at a pretty good clip. But, with the disappearing sunlight, the air started to get colder. Optimism waned as both the men's pace and dialogue gradually decelerated.

Soon, the speed of the blowing wind began to do just the opposite of the men's legs and mouths, and the temperature became bitterly cold. Conversations all went quiet, and the only lips that moved were caused by the chattering teeth behind them. The miserable silence felt as though it would never end.

~

"I've never been this cold in my life," Ella finally shouted out of exasperation.

"Me neither," Claire shouted back, giving herself a hug for

whatever warmth she could muster.

The movement of every single woman had slowed down as both their bodies and the snow they were trudging through continued to grow heavier, but they managed to deliberately advance despite the struggle.

"We can't keep this up for much longer," Shayal proclaimed between deep, heavy pants.

"We don't have a choice," Madison insisted.

Jill caught her breath before concurring. "That's right."

"There's always a choice," Ella chimed back in.

"Also right," Jill admitted.

"We can't give in." Madison doubled down as Jill continued to agree but chose to do so in silence.

"I'm pretty sure I could," Ella confessed.

"Enough of that chit-chat," Wanda shouted as she somehow managed to increase her speed. "Pull your big girl pants back up and mush, ladies!"

Ella, Claire, Shayal, and Madison all looked wide-eyed at Jill who shrugged her shoulders as she responded, "You heard her. Mush!"

~

As the snow began to fall and the headwind started to change direction, evolving into a forceful swirling motion, Kinsey wondered how long it had been since they left the caves. To him, it felt like it had been ten or twelve hours, but he was guessing it was more like seven or eight. In truth, it had been a little less than six. Kadosh had a funny way of messing with time. It always had.

~

All progress continued to slow as the wind blew harder and the snow, both on the ground and in the air, grew thicker and even heavier than they had ever experienced before. The inspirational boost that they felt after the previous day's victory that had been reinforced by the ice flowers earlier that morning had now eroded. Tatum believed it had been intentionally stolen by Raum, and she was right.

Determined that demonic influence would never overwhelm her, she tried to lead by example and force her body to trudge forward with the most haste she could drum up. She began to pass girls in her group, one by one, and they took notice. Gritting their teeth and furrowing their brows, they all pushed on to the best of their abilities.

Unfortunately, Raum was equally resolute and swiftly amplified his onslaught.

~

As the men faced white-out blizzard conditions, they were forced to stop and huddle up, yelling at one another just to make themselves heard over the howling wind.

"I can't do this anymore," Brandon was the first to admit. "I can't even feel my face."

"I'm with Brandon," Chris agreed. "We need to find shelter and wait this thing out. Can anyone see a cave or anything?"

The men all looked around. They were in the middle of a clearing and couldn't see more than about fifteen feet in front of them.

"All I see is white," Brandon announced.

"Let's head closer to the mountains and just keep going until we find something," Grant suggested. "Then we'll call it a night."

No one verbally agreed, but there were a few head nods, and everyone started moving in the same direction which was still a bit forward but primarily to the left of where they started. They stayed mostly huddled as they went slowly toward where they hoped a mountain to be, but it took about twenty minutes before a dark mass started to come into view.

~

"There," shouted Bryson, causing all the boys to look up and squint in an attempt to decipher what he was pointing toward.

"I see it," Logan added.

Trevor nodded his head as he concurred. "Me, too."

The boys made their way to the mountain in just a few minutes and walked along side it until finally arriving at a useable cave. It took almost an hour. The space was significantly tighter than the previous night's accommodations, and they were completely wiped out, but they were grateful, nevertheless.

The night was spent in an eerie quiet, another noticeable difference from the previous night. Everyone stayed focused on trying to get warm and remained introspective until finally falling asleep. If they were in a sporting match of some kind, they had taken round one, but round two had now gone to Raum. The victorious and hopeful attitudes they were experiencing the night before and even that same morning had eroded and had been replaced with a severe sense of discouragement.

Kinsey was sad to admit it to himself just before he drifted off, but he knew, wherever Raum was, he was smiling.

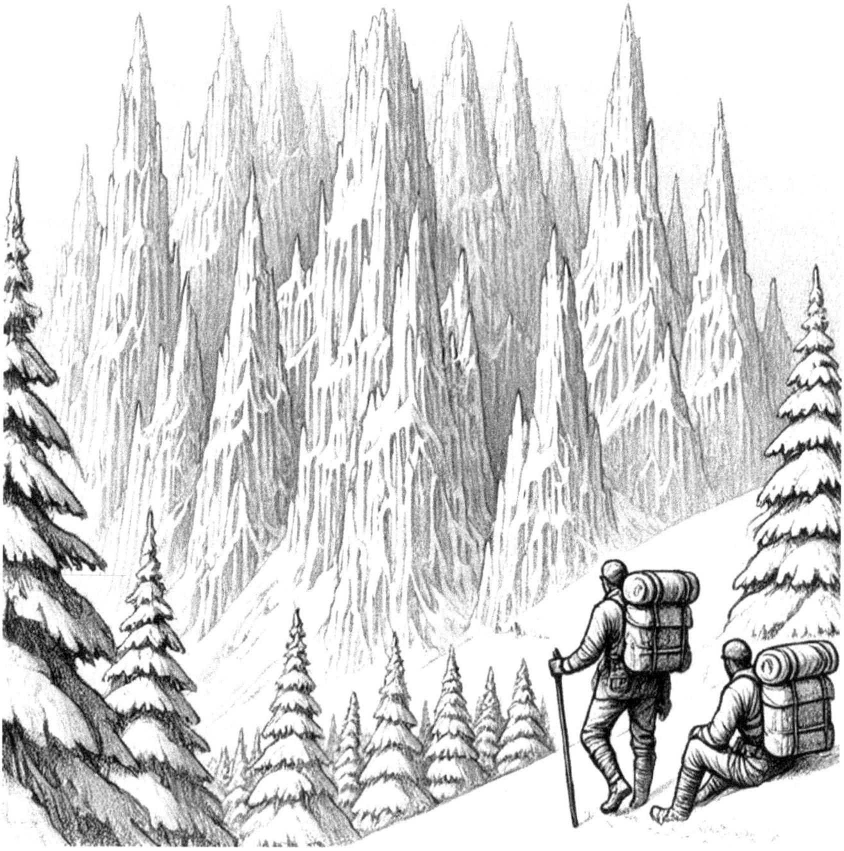

PART SEVEN
Hurdles

CHAPTER TWENTY-FOUR
Mood Swings

The weather had completely calmed overnight. Jill wondered if that was natural, if God had made it stop, or if Raum had given up because he had gotten what he wanted by forcing the group to pause their progress. Ultimately, she decided it didn't matter. It was a relief to wake up to silence and a visual confirmation of the landscape instead of howling wind and a total white out.

Unfortunately, the morning didn't remain as quiet as it started. It would have if it hadn't been for all the women waking up with moans and groans. Bodies were sore, and windburned skin was giving them a brutal stinging sensation. No words were spoken right away, but the sounds that were made, the body language that accompanied them, and the forlorn faces all spoke volumes.

~

Brandon was the first to utter actual words, and by doing so, opened the door for the list of understandable, however unhelpful, complaints. "I'm hungry. Maybe we should've brought more food."

"We brought everything we could carry," countered Victor.

"And we proved with the bears that we'll find more food as we go," added Grant.

"What do you say we make that a top priority today?" Brandon proposed.

"Fair enough," Grant agreed. "You just need to exercise some patience."

"Tell my bell-bell," Brandon said as he simultaneously rubbed his belly and let out a big yawn.

"I'm tired," Javier said as if Brandon had reminded him.

"Who isn't?" Ustav asked, garnering a few nods and chuckles including one from Brandon.

Grant turned and responded to Javier. "Can't help you there, buddy."

"Everything hurts," Dave added to the growing list and gained a lot of both verbal and physical agreement from the group, many of whom were in the middle of various stretches.

"Or there," Grant responded again, turning the other

direction and feeling the same pain everyone else felt with each movement. "Of course, I can't disagree, either."

"Maybe we should take a day off," Chris suggested.

"A day off?" Grant asked in disbelief.

"Yeah," Chris casually responded. "Just take a break."

~

"I can't do another blizzard," Kate admitted. "Not today. That was awful. I mean, really awful."

"I know, Kate." Tatum sighed deeply. "We were all there, and it was equally terrible for each of us. I can't argue with you."

"Is there going to be more?" asked Olive.

After another sigh, Tatum threw her hands up in the air and answered honestly. "Probably, yeah. Could be more of that, could be different stuff. Bottom line is this was never going to be easy."

"Well," Paris started to chime in, "we've certainly confirmed that truth."

"It was always going to be hard," Tatum continued, "and I'm just as beat up as you all are. But we have to keep going."

"How?" Fiona pleaded.

It was silent for a moment but then it was Ava who stepped up to the plate with a simple answer. "Hope and faith." Everyone, including Tatum, looked wide-eyed at Ava who simply shrugged her shoulders. "What else?"

~

"It's fine to rest at the end of the day," Kinsey started, "and to get to safety during a storm. Those are the right things to do. But we have to keep going when we can. We can't let up because Raum's not going to. We all made the decision to do this. So, let's do it."

There was a lot of quiet head nodding, but no one spoke.

~

"Ready to pack up and get out of here?" Grant asked the group. He scanned their faces and noticed more heads nodding, coupled with a few audible agreements. "Good, now let's go find Brandon something to eat before he turns into Bugs Bunny and we all start looking like a juicy steak.

~

The women moved quickly and headed back out on the quest to reach Raum's island. As they did, the muscles in their bodies began to loosen up and soreness became less of an aggravation.

The stinging in their skin from windburn, however, didn't seem to be letting up. Still, the general mood was more cheerful than it had been when they first awoke, and it felt like they were being rewarded with good weather.

It was still a long, albeit unusually uneventful by Kadoshian standards, day, and by the end of it, hunger had begun to deteriorate the mostly positive vibes. As sun began to set, they thought they were going to have to try and sleep with empty stomachs. Some wanted to go on the hunt, but the wisdom of finding shelter and building a fire before the temperatures plummeted won the evening. After all, nearly everyone there had known someone who had died of hypothermia in Kadosh, and several of them had experienced frostbite for themselves. The cold climate was not something to be trifled with.

~

Once again, the girls had found a cave system with plenty of room. As several of them began to build fires, the rest decided to explore and make sure there weren't any snow leopards or anything hiding somewhere that could prove to be a threat later in the night. The only group that found anything was Tatum's, and it wasn't much of a threat.

~

"Get Brandon," Grant told Chris without breaking his gaze. "This will make him very happy." He stared down at eight Arctic hares. He recognized them from their thick, brilliant-white fur and ears that were shorter than most rabbits. "God help me, they're cute, but they're also edible."

~

The boys were genuinely happier as they finished their meat. They were joking around and laughing. Of course, they also couldn't keep themselves from pondering what was going to come next on this roller coaster ride of an adventure. Kinsey knew that was a waste of time because there was no guessing what Raum would throw at them or when he would throw it. He began to turn his attention away from the group and suddenly noticed a green light coming from the mouth of the cave. Last he remembered, it had gotten completely dark out there, so he couldn't figure out where any light would be coming from that would be noticeable over the flicker of the fire. *What would make it green,* he added to his wonderment.

Without saying a word to anyone, he got to his feet and slowly walked toward it. As he did, he gradually realized that outside itself seemed to be glowing. As the other boys began to notice what he was doing, they stood up and followed him. He crept toward the cave's entrance and turned his head up to see the most brilliant light display he had witnessed besides his previous two journeys from home to Kadosh and the last return trip.

The sky was layered in what appeared to be translucent curtains made of a variety of colorful lights. The bottom layer was green that transitioned into yellow, then pink, then red, then ultraviolet, and ultimately topped out in a beautiful blue. It was absolutely spectacular, and unlike Kinsey, no one else had ever seen anything remotely like it.

~

Ava stood next to Tatum and stared at the magnificent display without even glancing at anyone or anything else. "That's incredible."

"Yeah," Tatum agreed, "it is. Just like the ice flowers."

"What do you mean?"

"God is encouraging us to keep going."

"I have no doubt."

"We can't be much more than a day away from the water."

"You mean the ice?"

"Right. The ice. Might even get there tomorrow."

"Just get us there. We're fully behind you and we'll face anything Raum sends our way. We're on the side of the light now."

Tatum smiled. Ava couldn't have been more dead on.

CHAPTER TWENTY-FIVE
All Who Wander

Jill got the group up early and headed out, hoping to make it to the spot where they had caught the boat that took them to Raum's island on the previous trips before the end of the day. Out front, she was walking and talking with Kate. As they had become accustomed to on this journey, they trudged through the powdery snow. It was so beautiful, untouched since falling and smoothed out by the wind, that it almost seemed criminal to mess it up with the unkempt trail they left behind them.

"What year was it when you left?" Jill asked the question without taking her eyes off the horizon.

"Left?" Kate chuckled. "That makes it sound like I had a choice. I know what you mean though. 1972."

"You've been here a long time."

"Yep," Kate acknowledged. "Any chance we get to go home

today?"

"Unlikely," Jill admitted. "I'm just hoping we make it to the water today. Or, ice, or whatever. To be honest, Kadosh has looked different every time I've been here, so I'm confident we're headed in the right direction, but where we are in relation to where we're going is a bit of mystery."

"Sounds like Kadosh to me."

"Exactly."

~

The boys began a steep climb up a hill that was buried in the snow, and the conversation quieted as breathing became a little more labor-intensive. As they finally reached the crest, Kinsey stopped to catch his breath. He let out a quick yell and threw his hands behind his head to open his lungs. "Woah!"

"No kidding," Connor agreed as he did the same.

Slowly, everyone reached the top of the hill and fanned out on both sides of Kinsey. The view was spectacular. The clearing they were in was outlined by humongous trees as far as the eye could see, and the path took a dogleg at the bottom of the hill they were standing on top of. Kinsey also took notice of the fact that the side they had just climbed up was covered in powdery snow, but the snow on the side they were now facing seemed flatter and more compacted. He wondered if the direction of the wind had caused the strange division.

"What are we waiting for?" shouted Micah from the end of the line to Kinsey's left. As Kinsey turned to answer, he saw Micah start to take a casual step forward and immediately slip. He fell to his back and began to slide down the hill.

"Wait," Kinsey shouted as he saw Connor reach out to try and rescue Micah who, by then, was already way too far gone. "Let's follow him down, but be careful. We don't need anyone getting hurt."

~

The men gingerly made their way down the long, steep hillside with only a few slips. When they did, they were finally able to view what waited for them around the dogleg of the clearing. They stood in silence, staring at thousands of massive ice-spires blocking their way and extending into the trees on both sides that were almost as tall as those same trees and even closer together. It almost looked like a gothic maze made of crystal. The sunlight beamed down and pierced the ice which split it up and sent it back out in multiple directions. The effect was mesmerizing.

"How do we get around that?" asked Dave.

"Can't tell how wide it is," Ustav responded. "Could go on forever as far as I can tell, just from looking at it. Might have to go through it."

Suddenly, an enormous albino moose came bounding out of the woods, turned its head to look at the group, then sauntered inside the immense cluster of ice-spires.

"That thing had to be close to two thousand pounds," Dave announced. "I've never seen anything like it."

"Well," Victor started ponderously, "if he can go through it, why can't we? Should we follow him?"

"I don't know," Grant answered honestly.

"Come on," Victor insisted. "Trying to find our way around this thing could take forever. This'll be way faster."

"But we don't know how to get out or what's waiting for us inside," Grant insisted.

"How bad could it be?" Javier asked with a bit of swagger. "That blanco moose seemed okay with it, and he's probably been in there lots of times."

"Let's vote," Grant suggested with a shrug of his shoulders. "Show of hands. Who wants to follow that white moose?" Grant watched as almost everyone raised their hand. "I guess we're goin' in."

~

Tatum led the group into the spires, determined to simply keep going in the same direction and hoping that they would eventually just come out on the other side. After about ten or twelve minutes, she suddenly spotted the moose less than forty feet away. It was staring at them, almost as if it had been waiting for them, and once eye contact was made, it turned and continued its journey.

Briefly, Tatum thought that this meant they were on the right trail. But then the moose started going at about a forty-five-degree angle instead of straight like she was hoping to do. "Now what?" she wondered out loud.

"That moose knows more than we do," Rebecca stated matter-of-factly. "I say we keep following it."

"It could be a trap," Tatum speculated, sounding exasperated.

"It's a moose," Irisa sneered, "just trying to get somewhere, and it's the closest thing we have to a guide."

"Yeah, that's exactly what worries me."

~

The women continued to follow and couldn't believe how long they had been inside the maze of spires. The moose had zigged and zagged to the point where they no longer had any idea which direction they were now going compared to the one they had started out in. They could have circled back near the beginning for all they knew at that point. Slowly but surely, they all found themselves getting increasingly tired and cranky, frustrated and scared.

Suddenly, the moose stopped, turned to look at the women, and shifted its body to face them head on.

"Is that thing going to charge us?" asked Claire.

Before anyone could respond, the moose's eyes turned a bright, glowing red. It quickly stood up on its hind legs, completely vertical, and its body, including all four limbs, transformed into something like a giant human. It's antlers, which started out looking like coral reef, rapidly converted into four, individual, sharp and protracted horns. As they turned from white to black, and the body kept its original bleached appearance, the creature grew a mane that looked like long, dark dreadlocks. The only thing that didn't change was its head and face area which still looked like a moose with those newly red eyes.

~

Fear nearly crippled the boys as they stared at the freakish, hideous monster, with no idea where to go or what to do. "It's a demon," Kinsey announced just before it grew massive wings, flapped them twice, and vanished in a puff of black smoke. "Or *was* a demon."

"Well, thank God it's gone!" exclaimed Xane.

"Now what do we do?" Ammon probed out of anxiety. "He's gone, but he got us lost first."

"Yeah," Micah joined in, "where are we?"

Everyone looked at Kinsey, hoping he would have the answer, but he didn't. He had no idea where in the ice-spire forest they were standing and even less of an idea how to get out. That moment was the first time since his first trip to Kadosh that he truly didn't know if he was going to make it back home. The boy who had taken a step toward Raum the first time he had faced the demon on his very own island, when everyone else was frozen in fear, suddenly found his faith tank on empty. And the one thing they all knew to be true was that, if Kinsey felt lost, they were in a lot of trouble.

CHAPTER TWENTY-SIX
Partly Cloudy

"Mustard seed," Kinsey whispered to himself.

"What?" Bryson asked, sincerely confused.

"Mustard seed," Kinsey repeated before clarifying. "If you have faith the size of a grain of mustard seed… We don't have to have all the faith in the world; we just have to have some. Grab each other's hands."

"Why?" Logan asked, just as confused as Bryson.

"We're going to pray."

~

Even the men who would typically scoff at the idea of prayer were desperate enough to have grabbed hands and bowed their heads. It wasn't the volume of faith that a fiery church's prayer meeting might produce, but faith was present and that's all God needed.

"Father," Grant began, "we need Your help. We're lost and afraid. Increase our faith and guide us out of here, the same way You guided the Israelites out of Egypt. Although, I have to ask You please not to let our journey to Raum's island last forty years. We can't do this on our own. Rescue us, God. Guide us. Deliver us. Get us home. Please. Thank you. In Your son Jesus' name we ask these things. All glory to You. Amen."

"Well?" inquired Ustav.

"Well, what?" Grant responded.

"Did He tell you how to get us out of here?"

Grant sighed. "That's not really how it works." He started looking around for some sort of sign or new idea.

"How does it work then?" Ustav was getting agitated.

"Just let me think," Grant insisted, continuing to scan the area but not seeing anything besides the same thick forest of massive upside-down icicles he was staring at before the prayer.

"Come on, man. How are we getting out of here? I don't want to die in a stupid frozen jungle."

"You think I do?" Grant finally snapped. "I didn't want to come in here in the first place. I was outvoted. Now that we're stuck in here, we have to believe God's going to guide us out and exercise a little more than two freaking seconds of patience while we wait to see how He chooses to do it. Is that too much to ask?"

The group stood in stunned silence until, out of nowhere, the sky above the spires darkened causing the light display created by the sunlight's impact on the spires to vanish. Everyone quickly looked up to see a dark cloud that had moved in above them and was actually descending toward them.

"What is that?" Javier asked on behalf of the entire group.

"Call me crazy," Grant began to respond, "but that might be a very literal answer to my prayer."

~

The girls watched as the cloud seemed to park right in front of them, hovering just above the ground and no longer blocking the sun from creating its beautiful display through the ice-spires. The tallest among them had to stand on their tippy toes to see over it. The others were just out of luck.

"What do we do now?" asked Yanna.

Suddenly, the cloud began to move away from them but stayed at the same height.

Tatum watched for about two seconds then turned to answer Yanna. "We follow it."

"How? We can't see past it."

"We don't have to."

~

As the cloud sailed through the ice-spires, the women wove their way around them in pursuit of it. Strangely, they noticed that the spires that went through the middle of the cloud were damp and less frosty than the others, as if they had melted only slightly by the time they reached them. Unable to determine why a cloud would have that effect on the ice, they decided to ignore it and focus on getting out of the maze.

The women assumed the route that the cloud had taken them was the most efficient because they found themselves on the other side of the forest of ice-spires and back in a clearing in what felt like about a half of an hour. They stopped to celebrate and breathe deep sighs of relief before even noticing that the cloud had also come to a halt precisely when they did.

~

"Why is it still here?" Trevor asked the question to no one in particular.

"Maybe it's going to keep leading us to Raum's island," Kinsey pondered out loud. He took a step toward the cloud and stopped again. It moved about the same distance he had. He repeated the process and so did the cloud. "Let's keep following it."

~

The men continued to track behind the cloud for another hour or so, growing weary along the way. Finally, Brandon posed the question on everyone's minds. "So, is this thing going to lead us to shelter for the night? Or, can we decide when it's time to take a break and hope that it waits for us?"

"I'm not exactly sure," Grant wondered verbally. "It did wait when we stopped earlier, but I don't want to quit before we're supposed to. Let's give it a little more time and then we'll figure out what to do."

"It's already been a long day, man." Chris chimed in with an exasperated look on his face that matched the tone in his voice. "How much is a little more time?"

"Excuse me!" interrupted a distant voice. "Hello! Excuse me, please and thank you very much!"

Everyone stopped and spun in all directions to try and locate the source of the voice. Finally, Dave spotted a squatty, East-Indian man running toward them from the woods to their right and hastily pointed him out. "There he is."

As the man closed in on the group, he couldn't wait to greet them. "My name is Marut and you have not a clue how happy I am to make your acquaintance. You are the first people I have seen since my arrival in this very strange place."

"How long have you been here, Marut?" Grant asked, extending a friendly hand.

Marut aggressively reached out and took Grant's hand with both of his, shaking it vigorously. "Oh, I have no way of knowing, sir. It was completely dark when I arrived and seemed to stay that way for a long time. Then the sun came out, and soon after, the snow began to fall."

"Years," Grant responded, surprised. "You've been here for several years. How have you survived?"

"Well, I have lost many pounds in the process, I can assure you."

"I'll bet. I'm Grant, by the way."

"Oh, the pleasure of meeting you is all mine, Mr. Grant. And you have friends. I am very pleased to meet all of you. Very pleased indeed."

Grant finally took his hand back. "Do you have shelter nearby, Marut? We're pretty wiped out."

~

The boys hadn't met anyone new, but they had managed to find shelter, build another roaring fire, and cook up a broth made from the last of the hare bones they had brought with them from the previous cave. Normally, this would be a time of spirited discussion, but everything was unusually quiet that night as they all stared outside of the cave at the cloud that was waiting for them to get their rest.

As night had fallen, the dark cloud that had contrasted so perfectly with the bright sun and white snow had slowly dissolved to reveal a burning pillar of fire that stood in equal contrast to the darkness of night. *God is amazing,* Kinsey thought to himself with a renewed sense of faith that was stronger than ever before. *Raum doesn't stand a chance.*

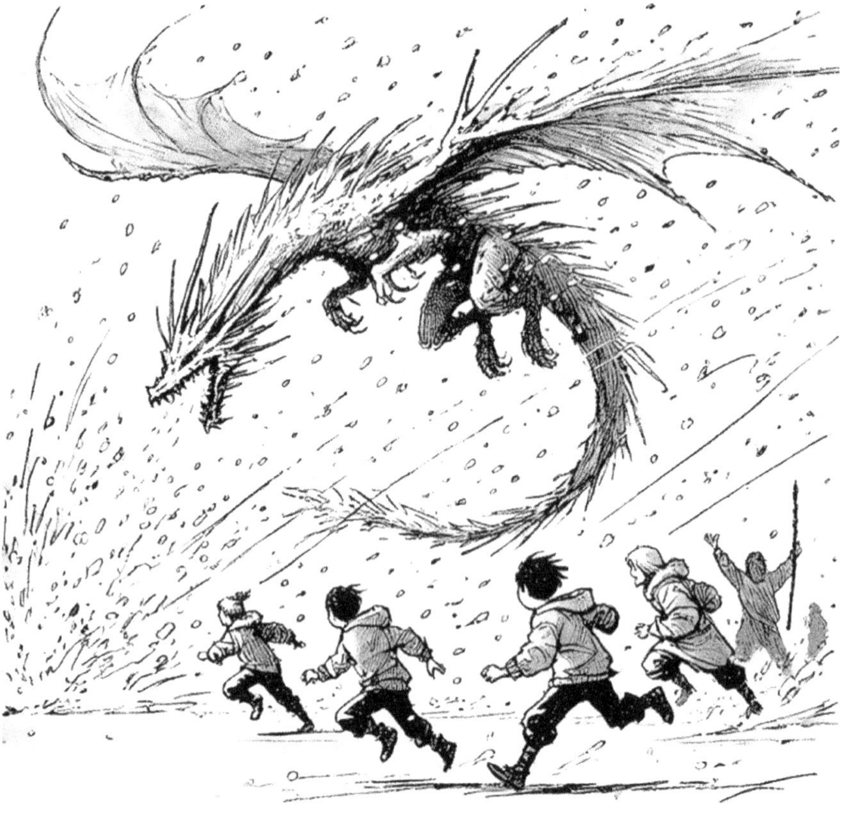

PART EIGHT
Ice Walkers

CHAPTER TWENTY-SEVEN
Glass

    As dawn began to shed its light on Kadosh, the burning pillar of fire that waited for the girls outside of their cave overnight began to disappear behind the thick, dark cloud that had surrounded it the day before, and the girls wasted very little time in following it, hoping that it would lead them to Raum's island.

    After a couple hours of walking, they came across their old camp. It was buried in snow, but the unusual shapes beneath the covering reminded those who had lived there of what was behind them in time. It was a somber moment, and very few words were spoken as they walked through it and then reached the point where the snow met the ice.

~

"It took about a day longer than I thought it would, but here we are." Jill stared at her feet and the spot directly in front of them where the surface of the ground she was standing on was about to be drastically different.

"What if we fall through?" Shayal asked.

Jill responded with a question of her own. "Do you want to get home and see your husband again?"

"Of course," Shayal quickly answered.

"There are no other options. This is the only way to make that happen. Besides, we're following the cloud. It hasn't steered us wrong yet. We can trust it to keep us on a solid path. As long as we don't deviate from that, we should be fine. We'll take it slow, okay?"

Shayal nodded in agreement just before Wanda zoomed right past them like an Olympic speed walker. "Move it or lose it, ladies."

~

"What's your wife's name?" Grant asked Marut as they began to walk gingerly across the frozen water which looked like a sheet of glass with a heavy dusting of snow scattered on top that would lift and twirl with each cold breeze that blew over it.

"Shayal," he responded in the melancholiest tone Grant had

heard from the typically gregarious man. "I've been gone so long."

"You have, but I've got some good news for you."

"What is it?

"You go back to the moment you left. When you get there, it will be like no time has passed."

Marut stopped and practically accosted Grant, giving him a giant hug.

"I thought you might like that," Grant said with a chuckle.

"This is most wonderful news. It will be as though I never left, except that I can be a better husband. I can be a better man." A contagious feeling of joy was nearly pouring out of him. "And this ice truly does feel solid." Marut bounced up and down to demonstrate his point.

"Careful," Grant said with a smile, trying to hide his inner cringe that deepened with the sound of each crackle. "We don't want to tempt fate."

"I am very happy with fate now that it has turned. Fate brought you to me and you are the only good thing that has happened to me since I arrived in this place. What did you call it?"

"Kadosh."

"Yes, Kadosh has been most unpleasant. Until now. Now we are on the journey home where we will make our lives better than they were before the dreadful Kadosh."

"You get it more than most, my new friend."

~

The boys continued to tread carefully as a menacing cracking sound that could be heard with every footstep was a constant reminder that they had put themselves in danger the moment they left land and decided to play penguin for the remainder of their expedition.

They purposely spread out so the pressure they were putting on the ice would be scattered across a large area rather than concentrating it in one smaller location or in a single-file line. They hoped that this haphazard formation would decrease their chances of an accident. But nothing was guaranteed. That would be true walking on ice anywhere but especially in Kadosh.

~

Trying to take her mind off her fear of falling through the ice, Yanna decided to strike up a conversation with Tatum by asking about another fear, but one that didn't loom nearly as close. "So, assuming we make it across this massive stretch of ice…"

"Which we will," Tatum reassured her.

"Right, of course. After that, what are we in for when we get to the island?"

"It hasn't exactly been the same each time, so it's hard to say. At least with any specifics. We're definitely in for a major battle though."

"Awesome," Yanna said, heavy on the sarcasm.

"Have you ever heard the expression 'God is good?'"

"God is good all the time and all the time God is good. Yeah, I've heard it."

"This is definitely a battle of good versus evil, and since we're on the side of good, God is with us. He's shown up both times I've been through this. He'll show up again. Knowing that gives us all the reason in the world to be hopeful instead of fearful."

"Thanks. That helps. There's still some fear, I'm not going to lie, but that does help."

~

Jill spun around when she heard a short squeal and a thud. Hoshi was lying on her back. "Are you okay?"

"I'm fine," Hoshi responded quickly. "Just slipped. I'll be okay," she finished as she slowly got back to her feet and continued to walk. It was the first of many slides and falls on the ice and not just for Hoshi.

~

Grant tried to get up on his tippy toes to see over the dark cloud in front of him. It was brief because he had both felt the slick surface below him and witnessed a couple of small mishaps, but it was enough to know that he could still only see white. It was everywhere. Without trees, it was void of color or contrast in front of him, behind him, on both sides, above him, and below him. The only things adding any contrast were the people he was traveling with and the cloud he had so much trouble seeing around. The worst part was, there were no other islands visible. It was clear that the journey ahead of them had a long way to go.

~

As conversations had progressed, the boys had slowly and unintentionally shifted from their original spread out, scattered, individual positions into small clusters that were still pretty well dispersed. Kinsey was up front talking to Connor.

"Pensacola, Florida," Connor answered.

"Panhandle, right?" Kinsey followed up.

"Yep."

"Sounds nice."

"Sounds really nice right about now."

"I'll bet."

"If I never see snow again, that'll be just fine with me."

"I get why you might feel that way right now," Kinsey acknowledged, "but I can't agree with you. I love the snow."

"I thought I would," Connor reflected. "I had never seen it until I got here. Now I've experienced enough to last a lifetime."

"Understood." A split second after Kinsey's response to Connor, the ice beneath their feet began to tremble ever so slightly. He felt the minor vibration, causing him to stop, and quickly noticed it was slowly increasing in intensity. "What is that?"

"What's what?" Connor asked as he stopped, too, turning around to face his new friend.

"You don't feel that?"

Connor furrowed his brow, concentrating. "Now I do. What the heck is it?"

"Everybody stop," Kinsey shouted. "Do you feel the ice moving?"

"Yeah," Trevor responded immediately. "What is it?"

"Earthquake?" Bryson guessed in a panic.

"No," Kinsey shot him down right away. "This is something else."

"Something else like what?" Logan joined in the inquiry.

Kinsey stared at the ice and suddenly spotted a moving substance beneath it. "Something alive."

CHAPTER TWENTY-EIGHT
Subzero

Tatum stared at the murky, fluid form as it appeared to slither beneath the surface. "I see it," she said loudly as she kept watching, trying to figure out what it was. "It's white like everything else around here, so it's hard to recognize what it is, but it's definitely moving." She slowly realized that the creature was surrounded by water and working its way through the ice and toward the surface. As it got closer, although she couldn't see the creature itself, it became increasingly obvious that it was quite large. "Clear the area," she said quietly before realizing she needed to shout to make sure everyone heard her. "Clear the area!"

Tatum started to back away, and the other girls all followed her lead as the cloud simply stopped in place, waiting just as it had while they slept. The girls' movement became more erratic and panicky as the ice's shaking increased in both violence and intensity and then began to crack. Just about everyone slipped and fell a few times as they tried to get away, but they all bounced up and kept moving.

Finally, the surface rippled and burst open between the girls and the cloud, sending chunks of ice, from miniscule to massive in size, flying all over the place. The girls dodged the onslaught of frozen debris, several of them shrieked, and they all continued to look on as their withdrawal hastened.

The creature's head had already disappeared back under the ice, but the middle of a white, serpentine body glided from one end of the opening it had created to the other.

~

The men continued to retreat, simultaneously gawking at the hole in the ice as a giant arm made of compacted snow reached out of it, spread its massive hand wide, and pounded down on top of the ice, digging its icicle-like claws in and gripping it for support. It followed up by doing the same with a second, a third, and finally a fourth. Then it pulled up, stretching the creature's long neck out and revealing the enormous tyrannosaurus-rex-shaped head which quickly tilted in the direction of the men. It opened its mouth to let out a booming roar, and when it did, it revealed four upper and four lower rows of icicle-teeth, each row jutting out in a different direction.

That thing could shred anything it got its mouth around, Grant thought.

~

Backpedaling with increasing speed, several of the women slipped on the ice and fell hard with a thud as hundreds of ice-spiders, whose bodies were at least two feet in length with legs between a foot and a foot and a half each, were pouring out of the hole in droves and immediately heading directly toward them. Their bodies were dark like one might expect from a spider, but appeared to be covered in an icy armor of sorts that muted the complexion.

What is the deal with spiders this time, Jill couldn't help but wonder as she thought back to the smoke-spiders they had faced shortly after her arrival. If the volume of these ice-born arachnids wasn't scary enough, a giant one that Jill was guessing was at least ten times the size of the others and was probably their mother, suddenly crawled out over its assumed babies and spread open its circular mouth, baring eight long, sharp, icicle teeth.

~

Kinsey stared at the sky as a giant dragon made entirely of ice soared straight up in the air above the boys, and instead of breathing fire like the boys expected, it showered them with a blanket of snow.

~

The colossal, serpent-like creature slithering its way toward the girls was unlike anything they had ever seen. It appeared to have an almost infinite number of heads, each smaller than the one housing it inside of its throat, and each with icicle teeth that were proportionate to the size of their head and mouth.

Tatum couldn't help but think back to the thousand-pound reticulated python she and the other girls had faced on her first trip to Kadosh. *This thing makes that first one look tame,* she silently told herself. *How in the world are we going to kill it?*

~

"Draw your weapons," Grant shouted as he pulled two spears off of a sled. While the other men showed an immense, but understandable, amount of fear, Grant's face displayed unwavering resolve.

~

The women went on the attack, striking the spiders with clubs and spears. Their icy outer shell cracked open with the first strike, and a second blow was required to kill them. But, one by one, that's exactly what the women were doing.

Suddenly, the mother opened her gigantic mouth and let out a piercing screech that made all of the women cringe.

~

The ice-dragon swooped over the group, diving and soaring as it spewed snow all over the boys. They threw spears, swung clubs, and shot arrows, but no one had managed to connect with the elusive beast yet.

Finally, Kinsey pulled out a slingshot and a rock. He loaded it up and pulled back, taking aim. As he let go, the corners of his mouth turned up in a smile. He watched the rock hurtle through the air and smack the dragon in the side of the head.

The ferocious dragon stopped, hovering in the air, and turned toward the source of the blow.

Kinsey's smile slowly faded.

~

The girls were throwing everything they had at the massive snake. They were hitting it, too. The blows just didn't seem to be slowing it down. Running chaotically, the girls were trying to get away from the slithering serpent and slipping all over the place in the process as their airborne weapons seemed to sail right through it.

"We need to start a fire," Tatum yelled.

"On ice?" Olive yelled back. "Is that wise?"

"I don't think we have a choice."

"Do we have time?"

"Actually, we just have to get to the cloud."

"Why?"

"Because there's already a fire burning in the middle of it."

~

"Circle back to the cloud!" Grant yelled his instructions as loud as he could while traversing the ice in a "C" pattern on his way to the mysterious gift that he knew had been sent straight from God.

Most of the men weren't sure why Grant had commanded the move, but they followed the orders anyway. The beast seemed confused by the sudden change in everyone's direction and reacted by standing straight up, spreading its arms out wide, opening its mouth to let out a thunderous roar, and then clinching its fists and banging on its chest like a four-armed gorilla.

~

Continuing to smash the biggest spiders they had ever seen, until their mother had crawled out of the hole, the women quickly made their way over to the cloud and surrounded it, forming a complete circle.

"Now what?" Madison asked with a desperate sense of urgency as she watched the mother-spider begin to move toward them.

~

The ice-dragon soared toward the boys with incredible speed.

"Now I go in," Kinsey announced as he grabbed a couple of unused torches from Quigley's sled and immediately stepped into the cloud.

The ice-dragon circled over the boys, spewing loads of snow all over them.

Kinsey kept walking, moving further into the cloud. As he did, it got darker until it was as dark as a cloudy night, and then started to get light again as he slowly began to feel an increasing amount of heat. Suddenly, the dragon's snow poured into the cloud, but the heat quickly melted it, and Kinsey was almost instantly drenched with water.

Worried that the torches wouldn't light, or that if they did, they would get put out again, he lunged forward and got as close to the flame as he could without getting burned. He pulled the torches back toward himself, saw that they were lit, and then immediately turned and hustled to get back out of the cloud.

Kinsey burst onto the scene, flaming torches in hand, and quickly began igniting the tips of all the weapons. "Let's light him up!"

CHAPTER TWENTY-NINE
Soul Survivors

Almost simultaneously letting loose with a slew of flaming arrows and spears, the women quickly reloaded as the mother-spider was instantly barraged. The resulting hideous screeching sound she made was even more offensive than the one the women had experienced moments earlier, but they couldn't shrink back or let their guards down in any way because the smaller spiders were still on the attack.

Madison thumped one with a fiery club, creating a burst of sparks before spinning in a circle and doing the same thing to three others. She kept the motion going and smashed all four of them like she was in an old arcade and playing a game of Whac-A-Mole.

~

Finally, the first of several arrows penetrated the roof of the beast's mouth and immediately began melting its icicle teeth. A guttural roar poured out of its throat as the beast reached up and started yanking the arrows out with all four hands. As he threw the third arrow to the ground, a spear that Brandon had thrown with an arc as beautiful as the perfect Hail Mary pass at the end of an American football game went straight down the beast's throat. Quickly, his hands raised back up, and he grabbed his neck, dropping to his knees as the energy quickly choked right out of him.

~

The ice-dragon coughed repeatedly. His ability to breathe snow was gone. In fact, his ability to breathe at all was vanishing and, with it, his life. Suddenly, it began to plumet toward the ice.

~

As the snake collapsed, it landed like a snowball, and the girls instantly knew that the wind would take care of the rest. They erupted in cheers, celebrating their victory over the vicious beast that Raum had unsuccessfully sent to stop their journey.

While the hugs and high-fives were peaking, Tatum glanced at the ground and, once again, saw something move below the ice. She did a double take, stopped, and stared at the ground. Everything around her fell silent as she focused in, wanting to know if either her mind was playing tricks on her, or the attack wasn't over.

~

"There's still something down there," Jill said, mostly to herself. But Wanda heard it.

"What did you say?"

"I saw something move."

Wanda looked at the ice, trying to figure out what Jill was reacting to. "I don't see…"

Suddenly, a barely visible face appeared beneath the ice.

"What the…" Wanda began to ask.

"There!" Jill shouted, causing everyone to turn and look as a semi-translucent fist began to pound underneath the ice. It was a horrifying sight. It appeared that someone was drowning, trapped beneath the ice. "Not again," Jill whispered, immediately realizing it was the spirits of those who had died on this same journey in the past. She had encountered them on each of the previous visits and knew that they still wanted to go home. *God,* she silently prayed, *tell me what to do. These people have broken my heart on each of my trips here. I want to take them with us, but it's too late for them. Tell me what you want. Tell me what to do.*

"Child," came a booming voice, grabbing everyone's attention in an instant. The women all spun in circles, trying to figure out where it had come from.

~

"Do you not know that I have the power to raise the dead?" The voice was coming from the cloud, and as they all realized it, everyone but Grant took a step away from the voice, most of them also glancing back at the spirit beneath the ice.

Grant stepped toward the cloud then took a knee and bowed his head in reverence as he remembered Kinsey's explanation of how the dry bones had turned into an army that helped them defeat Raum on the previous trip to Kadosh. "Of course you do, my Lord. I've seen it with my own eyes."

"But it is only those who have chosen to know me who will hear me when I call. Those who have chosen not to know me have sealed their eternal fate of isolation, fear, and self-inflicted torment. Bring them to me, and I will separate the wheat from the chaff."

"Yes, my Lord."

~

Kinsey stood back up and walked over to the spirit. He stared at him briefly before giving him a wave, telling him to follow. Kinsey started walking toward the hole in the ice that had been created by the dragon they had just defeated, and the spirit hovered under the ice, following his footsteps by swimming through the water.

~

Tatum stood just a few feet from the hole as the spirit of a girl who had died crawled out of it. She gave it another wave and walked back to the cloud. Behind the spirit, others began piling out of the hole in multitudes. Hundreds of spirits followed Tatum and hovered above the ice, waiting for their opportunity to finish the journey they had previously started.

~

It only took a moment before the atmosphere began to change. A dark cloud cover moved in and blotted out the sun.

Slowly, the cloud they had been following began to disappear, the same way it had before when night approached. The fire burning in the middle of it became visible again, and it was blazing. If it hadn't been for the fire, it would have been total darkness, but the flames provided a light so bright it was difficult to stare into.

Jill watched as some of the spirits began to shield themselves and back away almost instinctively. "Where are you going?" she whispered but didn't receive a response. She kept watching as more spirits retreated than the number who stayed. Noticing that those who backed away were trembling in fear while those who remained looked like they were experiencing the same comforting warmth she had first felt while encountering the light on Raum's island, a sadness crept over her, and tears began to stream down her face. *How could they turn down this opportunity?* she silently wondered. The question only lingered for a moment and was quickly replaced by the answer. These were the spirits who were doomed by a terminal decision made long ago before their deaths.

~

"Depart from me," came the resounding voice from within the fire, causing Grant to turn back around, "all those whom I never knew." He stared at the fire for a moment before returning his gaze to the spirits who were now fleeing in fear and quickly disappearing back into the same hole they had come out of.

~

With all that he and the Snyders had been through, both in Kadosh and back home, this was the deepest sadness that Kinsey had ever felt. The weight of witnessing the eternal consequences of choosing not to have a relationship with God brought with it a sorrow unlike anything he had ever experienced.

~

As the last of the souls that had been separated disappeared into the hole in the ice, the clouds in the sky began to clear, the sun came back out, and the cloud on the ground started to conceal the fire again. When the process was complete, the girls looked around at each other and quickly discovered that the souls who had stayed were no longer just spirits but had new bodies. They had been fully resurrected from the dead.

The sorrow that had weighed them all down just moments earlier quickly turned to joy and thankfulness as they celebrated the blessing that they were experiencing. Congratulatory, joyous hugs were exchanged, including a tight embrace between Kate and the friend she had lost, Natalie, the last time she tried to cross the ice.

While the festive mood continued, the journey wasn't over. So, the girls gathered their things and once again followed the cloud, ready to reach Raum's island. However, the demon was far from finished throwing up roadblocks.

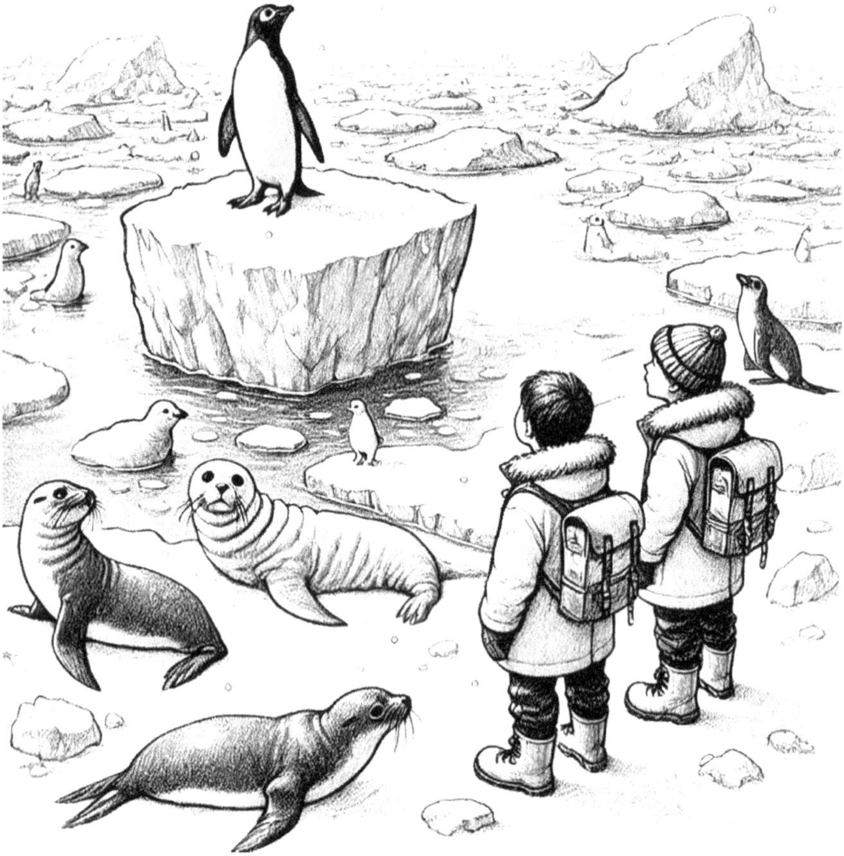

PART NINE
From Cold to Hot

CHAPTER THIRTY
Steam

The wind had picked up and was blowing the fallen snow across the ice so fast Kinsey thought it looked like he and the boys were intruding on some sort of race secretly known only within nature. The cold was bitter, and the conversation had gone silent again, but no one felt discouraged. The boys were all just as determined as they had ever been. Some of them did find themselves wondering how the cloud could seem unmoved by the fierce wind, but Kinsey reasoned that it made perfect sense when he included what he called the "God factor."

Within the natural order of things, a cloud would easily be carried away by a strong wind. But ever since his first trip to Kadosh, Kinsey had been seeing things through a different lens. The supernatural was very real, and this strange world had proven that to him. He remembered reading a verse in the Gospel of Matthew where Jesus had stated that "with God all things are possible," and that simple statement had caused what didn't previously make sense to click. The supernatural was just what the word implied; it was beyond natural. But that didn't make it any less real.

God existed in the supernatural realm. So did Kadosh and everything in it. The people who wound up there had previously only existed in the natural realm, but Kadosh, as horrible as it was, provided a chance to catch a glimpse of what was going on all around them at any given time, whether they were aware of it or not. That glimpse was a fascinating opportunity, but to recognize it for what it was, one had to first get past the fact that it was also terrifying.

~

The winds had become so fierce, blowing on the right side of the women, that everyone was forced into the strongest formation they could come up with. They had linked arms and were walking very slowly. Those carrying sleds had tied them to their waists, and everybody was having trouble staying vertical. They also had to stop every few minutes and let the woman taking the harshest beating rotate out of their position, allowing the next woman in line take their turn.

The sound of the howling wind was all they could hear, and the women feared that the only thing keeping them alive was the amount of effort they were being required to put into traveling. Like the boys, the women refused to allow discouragement to resurface because of the weather conditions. Still, they were all silently praying that, although they couldn't see it, Raum's island was mere steps away. They were worried that their bodies could give out at any moment. However, as Jill had learned a long time before this trip, in Kadosh, you had better be careful of what you wish for.

~

The men weren't faring any better than the women or the boys. No one would argue the fact that the weather was horrendous, and progress was happening at the most sluggish pace so far.

The first to collapse was Brandon. He was about halfway down the line, and suddenly, he just dropped, nearly taking Chris and Marut with him. The line stopped moving as the men on both of his sides picked him up, draped his arms over their shoulders, linked back up with the line, and continued to march forward.

It was an incident that began a bit of a domino effect as four more bodies gave out and men collapsed. Each were picked back up like Brandon was, and those who could carried the rest toward their destination.

Grant's realization and the announcement that followed couldn't have come at a more opportune time. "I think the wind is letting up!"

~

As Tatum's insight caused everyone to begin paying more attention to the possibility that conditions were improving rather than how bad they had been, spirits were raised, and the prospect was quickly confirmed. The weather did indeed get noticeably better, and with it, the pace began to pick back up, but the girls were exhausted and several of them were barely helping the line to advance.

While those who hadn't collapsed yet worked extra hard to make up for those who simply weren't able to even hold themselves up, the girls began to feel like they were walking out of the storm. The wind continued to dwindle until it had nearly stopped, and visibility changed with it but didn't exactly clear up.

"Is it just me or does anyone else suddenly not feel quite so much like a Klondike bar?" Ava asked. Without even realizing that no one responded, she continued her wonderment out loud. "Is this fog?"

~

"Yeah, I don't know when it changed from snow in the air to just foggy, but I think that's exactly what it did," Kinsey finally answered Connor as they continued to rally forward. Their feet felt heavy, and the ice beneath them was slippery, making the simple act of walking extremely laborious. Plus, they were following a cloud surrounded by thick fog, so visibility was practically non-existent. But the further they walked, the better the conditions became. In fact, the air continued to get warmer, which felt great at first. Slowly, however, it began to produce tiny beads of sweat on their exposed skin.

"It's starting to feel like home," Connor allowed his thoughts to fall through his lips.

"Yeah," Kinsey pondered with him, "humid, right?"

"Definitely," Connor agreed.

"In fact, what felt like fog you'd get at the beach now feels more like…"

"Steam?"

~

"Exactly," Jill confirmed. "How is that possible?"

"I've kind of stopped asking that question," Hoshi stated with a hint of exasperation.

"Fair point," Jill admitted, quietly realizing that she should have thought about the Kadosh element of the inquiry herself since she was a three-time-veteran.

As they continued to push through the exhaustion and the new way the atmospheric conditions were messing with them, they were able to stop linking arms and tried to make themselves as comfortable as they could, which wasn't really all that comfortable. They naturally began to spread out again and soon noticed that the visual limitations finally, slowly began to diminish. The distance they could see in front of them was steadily increasing, and they also started to hear an unfamiliar noise.

Madison was the first to acknowledge it out loud. "Do you hear that?"

It was a gentle, rhythmic sound, a kind of swishing, lapping reverberation. Jill finally answered Madison's question with one of her own. "Is that water?"

~

As the men continued to walk into clear air, visibility reached a maximum, and Raum's island finally came into view. What they saw was very black, but also included a strange, reddish glow scattered around it. While curious about exactly what they were seeing, they were a bit distracted by the excitement invoked by the revelation that their destination was finally close enough to be visible.

The distractions seemed to multiply as they got closer, too. The next one came as they realized the ice didn't go all the way to the island but began breaking up into floating patches up ahead of them, and there was a good amount of water separating the surface beneath their feet and the solid ground they were trying to reach.

The final distraction came as they started spotting wildlife. First, they noticed massive leopard seals lounging on ice floats and the shoreline. Then it was several flocks of arctic terns both in the sky and in the water, followed by emperor penguins who, like the seals, were hanging out on patches of ice and at the water's edge. Finally, it was both humpback and killer whales swimming separately in the water that stood as a roadblock between where they were and where they wanted to go.

The men stopped and stared straight ahead. No one spoke for what felt like several minutes until Ustav proposed a very simple question. "Now what?"

CHAPTER THIRTY-ONE
Unstable

"Did that fog somehow transport us to some kind of messed up version of the Wild Arctic section of Sea World?" Yanna deadpanned.

"Looks that way," Olive quickly responded. "Seals, penguins, whales… We've got the works."

"Were these things here when you got this far before?" Paris asked Tatum.

"No," Tatum answered honestly. "But Kadosh is always changing.

"So, what do we do now?" asked Fiona.

Suddenly, the cloud that had been leading the way floated out over the water and onto the shoreline of Raum's island where it stopped, waiting for the girls to follow.

"Same thing we've been doing," Tatum responded. "We

keep going.

~

Jill started walking, not even sure where she should look with the ice thinning and making cracking sounds beneath her feet and the vast wildlife all around her that she knew could pose a threat at any moment. The women marched with her, demonstrating the same trepidation. The artic terns in the sky began to circle overhead, quickly diverting the women's attention and causing their fear to increase dramatically.

~

As the boys approached the spot where the ice met the water separating them from the next floating patch nearby, they spotted another large chunk that looked more like a miniature iceberg. It was inhabited by seals who appeared to be starting to pay attention to the boys, which made them even more uncomfortable than they were already feeling.

Suddenly, one of the penguins waddled its way to the top of the mound in the middle of the ice and proceeded to intentionally nosedive from the peak, sliding down the side facing the boys and launching himself at them with extraordinary intensity.

The Four Corners of Winter

~

Quickly grabbing a club out of the quiver-like sack on Ustav's back, Dave swung it like a baseball bat and smacked the penguin in the head. It was like hitting a boxer's heavy bag. The bird's momentum carried it through, barely slowing down when the blow occurred, and it landed mostly on the ice near Dave with a thud followed quickly by cracking sounds from the impact on the ice. As part of the ice broke off and the body gave way to gravity, the whole thing slowly rolled into the water.

Dave stood back and watched with the other men as an orca tail emerged from the ocean beneath the penguin and flipped it back onto the ice. The men jumped away from it and then immediately turned to their left as they spotted another penguin in their peripheral vision sailing toward them from the same small iceberg the other one had come from. Two others were following right behind it.

~

As the girls continued clubbing penguins and knocking them into the water, the orcas began to circle the stunned birds, nudging them playfully at first before beginning to feast on them. Tatum stood back and wondered if that was simply nature taking its course, or if they, on behalf of Raum, were warning the girls that trying to get past the apex predators could cost them their lives.

~

"How are we supposed to get to the shoreline?" asked Hoshi.

There was a moment of silence as the women scanned the area. Madison responded with an idea first. "We're going to have to leapfrog it."

"We're going to have to what?" Shayal inquired in serious need of clarification.

"Treat the floating ice patches like lily pads," Madison insisted.

"Lily pads?" Shayal's questions persisted. "Are we supposed to be frogs?"

"That doesn't exactly sound stable," Ella added.

"It sounds like a good way to wind up in a whale buffet," Claire joined in.

"Well, unless someone has a better idea," Jill started before being interrupted by Wanda who simply leapt onto the patch of ice in front of and to the right of the women. "I guess that settles that. Ditch whatever you can't carry." Jill followed Wanda's lead. The other women gave in amidst a few sighs and hurried to catch up.

~

Balancing on the ice patches added another layer of difficulty to an already perplexing situation. The water the ice was floating on was, obviously, fluid, and it was impossible to get the weight distribution from the women's bodies even. Plus, every time someone moved, it threw everyone else off balance. It would have been tricky enough if that was all they had to worry about, but the circling whales were also terrifying. Then it got worse.

Thankfully, the women were still holding their weapons when the terns began to divebomb them from the skies above. Unfortunately, swinging those weapons to knock the birds out of the air created a platform less stable than an active bouncy house.

~

Ammon was the first boy to fall into the water. He immediately tried to climb back onto the floating ice but couldn't get a grip and just kept slipping back off and under the water. Finally, Logan grabbed his arm, but when Logan tried to lift him up, the platform shifted, and Logan took an unexpected dive right over Ammon and plunged into the water.

~

Leaping to the next patch of ice, Grant suddenly found himself all alone, watching several more men fall into the water, trying to stay afloat while continuing to battle the attacking terns. He felt helpless. Panic set in as he silently debated the idea of jumping in himself. But then he saw Brandon give up on the ice they had all previously been on and start swimming toward him.

Grant laid down on his belly with so much adrenaline pumping through his veins he didn't even think about how cold the ice was. He stretched his arm out and waited impatiently for Brandon to reach him. Just before he did, Grant spotted one of the massive humpback whales swimming just beneath them. His eyes went wide about half a second before he felt Brandon's hand grab onto his.

While pulling Brandon onto the ice, he realized that more men were swimming right behind him. "Pull the next guy up, tell him to do the same for the guy behind him, then follow me." As soon as Grant was done shouting his orders, he got to his feet and scanned the area for his next "lily pad."

~

Tatum landed on the smallest patch of ice so far. She slipped a few times and had to use her hands while stabilizing herself. When she finally did, she looked up and had the largest leopard seal she had ever seen staring back at her from about three feet away. The seal quickly growled and slapped its flippers.

Ava was the next girl to successfully board the ice float and spot the seal. She and Tatum didn't speak a word; they simply stared the seal down and raised their clubs, ready for whatever came next. To their surprise, the seal let out one more growl and then slipped into the water.

~

The next leap was just barely too far, and Jill missed, plunging beneath the surface. Thankfully, it likely would have been the last leap anyway as the women had made it most of the distance to the island. Jill was close enough that she decided to swim for the shore. *Somehow, we always end up wet before we get to Raum's island*, she thought as she hurried toward the shoreline. Soon, she was able to put her feet on the ground and jog the rest of the way.

Turning around, she watched the other women rush toward her. Mercifully, the wildlife seemed to have given up and were ultimately leaving them alone. Unfortunately, she knew that didn't mean the hard stuff was over. The worst was yet to come. They were likely only moments away from facing Raum. As she accepted this, she looked up in the sky and realized that the sun had started to set. Much like her previous experience in Kadosh, she was about to climb the hill while mentally preparing to take the demon on in the dark.

CHAPTER THIRTY-TWO
Heat

With all the boys now gathered on the shoreline, Kinsey, following the cloud, led them up the embankment in search of their families. Those who had been there were reminded of certain beaches in Hawaii as they scaled the black lava rocks. Anticipation mounted and fear of the unknown increased for everyone except Kinsey.

Even with everything that was going on and all that he was anticipating, Kinsey couldn't help but let his mind drift a bit as he climbed his way toward the top. Following the cloud, along with the time he had accumulated in Kadosh, had proven what he had read in David's psalms. *There is no place we can go where God is not already there*, he thought to himself. The realization was an inescapable fact and, for Kinsey, as it should be for everyone who knows God in a personal way, a comforting one.

He welcomed the reassurance and the security that came with it as they neared the crest, and as they did, each of them noticed another sudden jump in temperature. Some of the boys had been almost constantly cold for years, so when they experienced the excessive warmth, it stung their skin. Yet somehow, it was more of a good feeling than a bad one. At least it was at first. Kinsey didn't remember the borderline feverishness feeling from his previous trips and wondered if things would look different when he landed on level ground. He was right.

As the boys finally reached the top and spread out into a single-file line with their backs facing the icy waters, they quickly began to perspire. They watched as the cloud lifted off the ground about ten feet higher than it usually hovered so that they could see the terrain. They stood motionless, staring out at an island that barely resembled what Kinsey remembered.

It was still clear, even from the topography beyond the embankment, that it had previously been covered in black lava rock because a lot of that rock was still there in its original form. However, most of it had been deconstructed into, and then covered in, red-hot lava that was still flowing and continuing to change the landscape. He finally understood why the island had been giving off the red glow.

Kinsey's mind first drifted back to images he had seen of

active volcanoes in Hawaii, South America, and Iceland. Suddenly, he remembered the fight scene at the end of *Star Wars: Episode III – Revenge of the Sith* where Obi-Wan Kenobi and Anakin Skywalker dueled on the planet Mustafar, a volcanic hellscape, and that was exactly what Raum's island had become. If it wasn't so devastatingly hot and frightening, it might have been beautiful in its own way. The lava had carved out streams and rivers, elegantly coursing with red magma, and there was a massive lava-dome in the center that spewed the liquid rock at least sixty-five feet above ground level as if it were a demonic fountain. It was like nothing any of them had ever seen before.

After a couple minutes of silence, Connor was the first one to speak. "You did not tell us about this."

"Nope," Kinsey admitted before explaining, "that's because, in true Kadosh fashion, this is very, very new."

~

"Where's Raum?" Brandon asked.

"Probably somewhere underneath the surface," Grant responded. "For now, anyway. He'll show up. You don't have to worry about that."

"Well, I wasn't exactly looking forward to it."

"No, me neither. Although, I am anxious to get this over

with and go home."

"I hear that," Brandon agreed before adding to his line of questioning. "What happens when he gets here? We take whatever he throws at us and go to battle?"

"Pretty much. The good news though, is that we won't have to do it alone."

"Great, but how are we supposed battle here?"

"Got to admit, I was just wondering the same thing."

Brandon wasn't exactly satisfied with Grant's answer, but he accepted that it was all he had in the moment. The two of them, along with the rest of the men, stared at their surroundings in silence for a full minute before noticing that the cloud was descending. However, instead of just going back to its original position, it lowered closer to the ground than it had ever been and then began to spread out into a longer, narrower shape of itself. It finally settled just above the men's waist-level, forming a fence-like barrier between them and the dangerous terrain they were facing.

"Well," Grant thought out loud, finally building on his response to Brandon, "I guess we stay put for now."

~

While the daylight was fading, further amplifying the light

created by the fiery liquid magma surging through the island, the girls finally began to look beyond their own group. They first noticed that the cloud was extending well beyond them and then realized that it was circling the entire island, creating a perimeter. What they didn't know then was that the four clouds that had been guiding the different groups had merged to become a single, unified entity.

They were standing behind the cloud like it was a guardrail at a national park when Tatum began to notice the other people, also standing behind it, on the other three sides of the island. "They're here!" she shouted with delight in her voice.

"Who?" asked Fiona.

"Our families," came Tatum's response, her voice now overflowing with both relief and joy.

"I see them, too!" Paris practically screamed with excitement as hope spread among the girls like wildfire.

Everyone started jumping up and down, waving their hands enthusiastically, even though the distance was so great and the light was so dim that no one could tell specifically who anyone in the other groups were. However, a euphoric sense of optimism had completely taken over. They wished they could sprint to one another and embrace, but there was still so much standing in their way. The agony of being separated had grown for each of them since their arrival in Kadosh, but it now ballooned exponentially because they were so close to reuniting and unable to finish the journey.

The more they moved and the more time they spent exposed to the heat of Raum's island, the heavier their sweat became. Their zeal didn't wane, but their energy soon did. They returned to stillness at about the same time the sun finished setting. With the onset of darkness, the cloud that had taken the form of a pseudo-guardrail around the entire island was slowly replaced by a line of small fires that burned like free-floating torches, serving as a perimeter from heaven, meant to protect the Snyders and their fellow travelers from an entire island inundated with the fires of Raum who had been sent from hell. And the demon was about to rise to the burning surface.

CHAPTER THIRTY-THREE
Hell Spawn

Although his surroundings looked different, the nervous feeling that settled in Kinsey's stomach was all too familiar. So was the hideous stink that had caused the nausea the second it saturated the island, right after the ground had begun to shake. Looking around, he quickly noticed that he wasn't the only one fighting both to keep his balance and plug his nose.

"Oh! What is that?" Connor asked, scrunching up his face to defend himself from the invasive attack on his senses as he thrust his arms out and widened his stance. "I can taste it. How is that even possible? It's like it went in through my nose and somehow ended up in my mouth."

The stench made everyone queasy. It was worse than any rotten garbage any of them had ever smelled. And, just as it had before, it got stronger as the ground shook, opened, and let more filth escape. The intense heat wasn't helping matters either.

Adding to the universal urge to barf was the rollicking surface everyone was standing on. Not only were they forced to endure the foul evidence of Raum's approach, but they had to do it while trying to stay vertical on what felt like a small sailboat traversing stormy seas.

Logan suddenly wished he could take a dose of Dramamine but quickly realized it would have to be a non-drowsy version because he needed to be fully alert for the events about to take place. Almost every thought he'd been having suddenly vanished because he was the first to puke and could focus on nothing else.

The sudden discharge caused a chain-reaction that affected nearly everyone. In fact, it essentially began a circle of projectile vomiting that spanned the circumference of the island.

~

One of the few not emancipating their previous meal from the depths of his stomach, Grant couldn't help but be reminded of a classic R-rated movie he had decided not to show his kids, mostly because of the foul language. In *Stand by Me*, there was a scene involving a blueberry pie eating contest that ended in an iconic mass-spewing event dubbed "The Barf-O-Rama," unlike anything that Grant thought he would ever have to witness. Yet here he was in Kadosh watching something very similar take place in an extravagant fashion.

~

It didn't surprise Kinsey that the high volume of exposed stomach contents had failed to improve the odor, but the fact that they didn't make it any worse confirmed just how bad the original fragrance had been. Suddenly, he remembered waking up on Thanksgiving morning, about a month before leaving for Kadosh, and how wonderful the house had smelled. *What a contrast,* he thought to himself as he compared his memory with the repugnant bouquet filling his nostrils in that moment. His longing for home hadn't been so strong since his first trip to the loneliest place he had ever known. *Alright, Raum, let's finish this.*

~

The shaking ground had a brief reprieve as Raum suddenly burst through the center of the bubbly, glowing orb of gushing lava in the middle of the island. He bounded through the air, spread his massive wings as wide as they would go, and dripped hot, liquid magma all over the terrain beneath him. Flapping his wings, the monster took flight, making a loud thrashing sound as he sailed over the men who jumped out of the way to avoid getting burned by his big, gloppy drops of lava.

~

Raum soared beyond the coast and circled the island, nearly flying in a zig-zag pattern as he tilted back and forth, purposefully dripping lava on the floating patches of ice and melting them to ensure that the people who had invaded his domain were left with no way of escaping it. In a complete disregard for the value of life, Raum didn't even consider the fact that a number of those patches of ice were occupied by seals and penguins who were quickly burned to death. It didn't matter to him in the slightest that they had served him in trying to stop the invaders who had caused his fury. Raum was the picture of selfishness, and selfishness has no integrity.

He glided his way back over the girls, causing them to dodge falling lava the same way the men had, and finally landed on solid ground with a resounding thud that once again shook the island. His foreboding stature was undeniable, and the entrance he had just made greatly emphasized that fact. In this world, his appearance as lord over all was irrefutable and effectively uncontested.

Tatum stared at the colossal, five-horned demon. He still appeared to be made mostly of the same black lava rock that covered the island, but the glowing red magma was running all over his body like blood in veins on the outside, even as more of it that was left over from the dome he had shot out of continued to drop off him.

~

His eyes were like balls of flickering fire as he scanned the faces of everyone who had dared to defy him. He finally settled on Kinsey, instantly recognizing the longstanding foe. His round mouth opened to show thousands of triangular teeth just before it released a violent roar and a stream of fire that looked like it had been shot out of a military flame-thrower.

~

"This is so much worse than anything I could have possibly imagined," Hoshi announced.

"Like Kadosh," Jill began to respond, "Raum is physically a little different every time. But in each way that matters, he's always the same evil beast."

"Is that supposed to be comforting?" Hoshi asked with a tone of exasperation.

"No," Jill answered honestly, "just factual."

~

Grant looked on, continuing to hold both his mouth and his nose even though he could still smell the awful stench that came with Raum's presence right through his fist. He watched closely as the monster stared down at his son. It didn't surprise him, but it made him angry and deeply concerned. He felt protective but knew there was nothing he could do himself to guard Kinsey. On his own, he was powerless. Thankfully, he wasn't on his own. In fact, he had access to the true Lord over everything, including Kadosh. So he began to pray, appealing to the only One who could actually keep his son, and everyone else on the island, safe.

They needed God to show up, and those who had been there before had no reason to doubt that He would do exactly that.

CHAPTER THIRTY-FOUR
Heaven Scent

The anxiety was palpable around the island but hope slowly began to push it out in the strangest of ways. The foul odor that had caused most of the people there to retch deliberately started dissipating. That revelation quickly caught the attention of the Snyder family. They knew from experience that when the dreadful smell of Raum disappeared, it was soon replaced by something wonderful which meant that God was sending help. Grant specifically recognized that the foul scent diminishing signified the answer to his prayers, and he couldn't help but smile in anticipation.

~

Sure enough, the familiar waft of exotic spices began to fill the air. For the first time in his experience, Kinsey was able to pinpoint one of them. He explicitly smelled jasmine, and it was intoxicating. He pulled his hand away from his face, uncuffed it, dropped his arms to his sides, closed his eyes, and breathed in deeply as the heavenly aroma burst into his nostrils.

~

Those with their eyes open suddenly noticed a light in the sky that hadn't been there just a moment earlier. They pointed and wondered out loud. It was unlike anything they had ever witnessed, as though darkness itself was being ripped open by the light which stood out in stark contrast. It was pure white against a black backdrop.

The Snyders were the only ones who had seen this before, but it appeared smaller and less dramatic than it had the last time. Previously, it had turned night into day. On this occasion, it seemed to assault the darkness while existing within the night.

Jill briefly pondered the likelihood that the reason for the difference was the fact that it had formerly restored Kadosh to its natural state, bringing daylight back after years of perpetual darkness. She further wondered if that meant it was about to melt all the snow and ice, but little did she know that God, whose ways are not ours, had other plans.

Raum spotted the light as well. He turned to watch as the source of the light approached, intensifying his anger. He roared and discharged a stream of fire as if he could reach the light and burn it out, but no matter how hard he pushed, it wouldn't go high enough.

Continuing its slow descent, the light floated from the stars toward Raum's island. As it neared, it became clearer that it was another cloud, glowing the brightest, purest white that any of them had ever seen. And they had just spent a significant amount of time in a world painted mostly white.

The closer it got, the more the warm breeze could be felt. It was like a lighter version of the air movement caused by helicopter blades, but the heat made it feel more like the gentle gust from a hairdryer being held above their heads.

The large cloud finally settled in the sky just beyond the reach of Raum's blazing wrath, although he continued to try to hit it. He even grew so frustrated and angry that he beat his chest, reminding Grant of a scene from a King Kong movie he had watched a while back.

Finally, Raum gave up but pouted about it and let out several additional grunts that could be heard by everyone on the island. He even kicked a big lava rock, sending it through the air about forty feet or so before it finally smashed into an even bigger one and shattered into about a hundred pieces. *Huh*, Grant thought to himself, *I guess the demon is just a big, obstinate toddler.*

~

Kinsey studied the cloud, and even from such a distance, he could tell that it was flowing with electricity. It coursed all over and throughout it. The cloud actually seemed to be alive.

Although he couldn't see inside of it, he remembered the four mostly humanoid creatures with shimmering skin he had seen inside the cloud the first time he was on Raum's island, and he assumed they were in there again. They had four faces above their shoulders. One was human, another was eagle-like, and on either side of those, the third was like that of a lion, and the fourth resembled an ox. They each had four wings, human hands, legs without knees, and stood on their hooves. He recalled thinking that they moved like lightning bolts and considered the possibility that their movement was causing the coursing electricity he was seeing on the outside of the cloud.

Kinsey also remembered that he had been the only one able to look directly at it the first time. At least initially. But after a moment, even he had to avert his gaze, and no one was able to keep their eyes open when it changed the night into day. This time, everyone was watching the cloud. He considered the prospect that the reason this was possible at that moment was the fact that the cloud was still further away than it had been when it arrived in the past. He wondered if and when it would come closer to outfit them with the armor it had blessed him and the others with on the previous two visits. But what he couldn't possibly know, was that the cloud was carrying an entirely different passenger, and events that were about to take place were not going to be anything like what the Snyders had experienced before.

PART TEN
The Last Battle

CHAPTER THIRTY-FIVE
Tarry

Gradually, everyone took notice of the fact that the new cloud had completely stopped descending, and there was no sign of that changing. It was as if a cosmic pause button had been pressed. Other than the consistent observation that the cloud appeared to be coursing with electricity, it no longer seemed to be doing anything at all. Even when Raum repeatedly shot fire at it, threw huge rocks in its direction, and stomped around in a huff because of it, the cloud just sat there motionless and altogether very decisively unresponsive.

Fiona was the first to question the lack of progress out loud. "I thought the cloud was supposed to come down and outfit us for battle."

"It usually does," Tatum responded, just as perplexed as everyone else.

"Then what's it doing?"

"I don't know."

"It's not doing anything," Olive chimed in. "That's the problem.

"Maybe it's waiting," Tatum tried to reason.

"Raum is right there," Fiona stated with some attitude. "So waiting for what, exactly?"

"I don't know," Tatum admitted.

"But you're the one that's supposed to have the answers," Paris piled on. "No one else has been through this before. So why does 'I don't know' seem to be your new pat answer?"

"I'm just being honest," Tatum defended herself before attempting to do the same for the cloud. "We needed God to show up and there He is."

~

"Yeah," Hoshi exclaimed, "way the heck up there. A lot of good that does us. We ditched the majority of our weapons, and you promised the cloud would outfit us for the battle. What's that look like, by the way? You never got specific on what that armor is."

Jill remembered seeing the ensemble on her body for the first time and how empowering it was. "It's a lot like the battle armor of a two-thousand-year-old Roman solider, I guess. Helmet, breastplate, shield, the works."

"I can see how that would be useful right now," Hoshi stated with a heavy dose of defiance. "That'd be really nice, but how exactly can that happen when the cloud is nowhere near us and doing absolutely nothing but observing? God showed up alright. But for what? To watch us die?"

"I hear you," Jill began to respond, "and you're not wrong. The cloud usually comes down and gives us our armor but then it leaves. Now it's staying. Something is definitely different this time, but it didn't come all this way so that God could watch us die. It's here to help us. I couldn't be more certain about that. I just don't know what the plan is or how it's all going to go down."

"Of course you don't."

"I'm sorry. I wish I could explain. All I know is that the cloud is here to help us defeat Raum."

"Again, how's it going to do that from all the way up there?"

"I'm not sure."

"Then how can you say you know it's going to help at all?"

"Experience."

"Your experience was that the cloud came down here," Ella jumped in to throw fuel on the dumpster fire of doubt. "That's not what's happening, so forgive me for not trusting your experience."

"I'll admit that my experience on this island in the past is no longer specific to this exact situation," Grant shot back, "but it is specific to the One in charge of it. The same One, by the way, that's in charge of that cloud up there. So, while I don't know *how*, I do know *Who*. And so do you to a certain extent. You've experienced some of the same things that I have. Who do you think was telling us He was with us when we woke up to the ice flowers? Or that amazing, colorful light display we saw the other night? And who do you think sent us the cloud when we were lost in the ice spires that led us out, carried us safely across the ice, and got us to where we are now? To not trust my experience, and for you to not trust your experience with God would be foolish and stupid. I have no doubt that He is here to help, and you shouldn't either. God won't leave us hanging. Trust me. More importantly, trust Him."

The men grew quiet as their attention shifted from Grant, back to the cloud, and then gradually settled on Raum who was still pitching a fit over his lack of ability to successfully lash out at the cloud. The men watched as, like their own fluctuating attentiveness, they observed the physical manifestation of Raum's evolving thought process. He had been focused on trying to attack the cloud, but that had proven unsuccessful. Suddenly, he realized that, while he couldn't directly damage the cloud, he could go about it indirectly by attacking something the cloud evidently cared about. It had come to rescue the people on his island, so he would have to settle for destroying them instead.

Raum once again scanned the faces of the people surrounding the edges of his island. Then, he suddenly bent down and ripped a massive piece of lava rock right out of the ground, lifted it over his head, spun around, and smashed it to pieces on the otherwise unaffected ground immediately before him. He beat his chest like he had before, but instead of breathing fire, he then bellowed the first word anyone there had ever heard him utter.

"Legion!"

~

"You didn't tell me that thing could speak," Connor said out of the side of his mouth in Kinsey's direction.

"I had no idea," Kinsey admitted.

"What do you think he means by 'legion?'"

"I think he's calling for reinforcements."

"Reinforcements? What's that mean? That can't be good."

"Nope."

Kinsey's theory was proven right as, almost instantly, all over the island, long, bony hands began to emerge from the flowing, hot lava and reach out to the rocky surroundings. The arms slowly pulled the bodies they were attached to out of the liquid and onto solid ground.

"Oh crud," Logan muttered. "What are those things?"

"Demons," Kinsey answered with little emotion.

These weren't like the demon they had seen revealed out of the moose in the ice-spire forest before. They were more humanoid, yet also far more hideous. Their emaciated bodies were lengthy, like they had been created tall and bipedal but had since been forced to use all four limbs to move across the ground. They had long, stringy, black hair clinging to their heads and bodies. The color of their eyes matched the lava dripping off them which burned their skin, but they didn't seem to notice or show any sign of caring. The worst thing about the creatures was that there were thousands of them.

"What are we supposed to do?" Quigly asked in a panic without taking his eyes off of Raum's legion.

"Gather whatever weapons we have left," Kinsey responded.

"What happened to 'the cloud will save us?'" Dave asked, looking directly at Kinsey with exasperation both on his face and in his voice.

"I still believe that, but it doesn't mean we shouldn't be prepared to use what we have in the meantime."

The Four Corners of Winter

The boys started pulling out every weapon they could find as the demons began to slowly approach. It was the same scene all around the island. As the internal battle between faith and fear continued to be waged in the hearts of everyone there, the floating fireballs began to expand and contract in perfectly synchronized intervals like it was the result of heavy breathing from a singular living organism. While fear was the more obvious of the two in that moment, faith was about to show everyone what it was made of.

CHAPTER THIRTY-SIX
Legions

"What is happening with the flames?" Marut pointed to the floating ball of fire closest to him as he asked the question, sincerely bewildered. This caused the men to look at it, followed by all the others of its kind to confirm that the event was consistent island-wide, and everyone silently wondered the same thing.

Suddenly, they all gasped and their bodies jerked in reaction to, upon each of the fireballs' expansions, something large simultaneously shooting out of them. Before they could even see what the big items were, more of them blasted out behind the first round, and the event persisted, rapidly repeating itself with each expansion. At the same time, the cloud above the island gradually increased in luminance until it acted like one giant floodlight, illuminating the entire island like a sports field at night.

As the men got over the initial shock of witnessing the flames turn into blazing portals, they began to realize that what had shot out of them was what ultimately appeared to be thousands of tall, athletic soldiers, dressed very similarly to the way the Snyders had described the people previously being outfitted by the cloud and armed with swords, ready for battle.

"Angels," Grant said out loud, more in awe than actually trying to communicate with anyone. "God sent his angels to fight for us."

~

Without looking away from the incredible sight in front of her, Hoshi couldn't help but admit her changed opinion to Jill. "Okay. Okay, you were right. I believe you."

Jill was so focused on the scene, Hoshi's words barely registered with her. She stared at one of the angels, evaluating his armor from head to toe. She first looked at the silver-colored, metal helmet he wore, slowly reaching her hands up to her own head and remembering what it was like to wear one herself. She then lowered both her gaze and her hands, crossing her arms in the process, and placed them between her chest and shoulders, considering the lack of weight she felt in that moment by not having the helmet on her head or the breastplate on her body.

Uncrossing her arms, she slid her hands over her waist and touched the belt she had on. It was far less substantial than both the one the angel was wearing and the one she had received from the light. She looked at the angel's sandals, then down at her own feet. Her storebought shoes seemed worthless compared to the ones she had worn at her previous two battles on the island. Her eyes then lifted, and she observed the angel again as well as the items he was holding before then regarding her own empty hands. She missed the sword and the shield that had previously occupied them, but far more than that, she deeply missed the warmth she had felt while accepting her armor.

Jill looked up again, finally noticing that the angels had formed a barrier between the people and the demons, who had initially shrunk back, but quickly grew violently angry with their timeless enemies and swiftly went on the attack. Raum's forces picked up rocks and hurled them at the angels while also breathing fire on a smaller scale but similar to what their leader had already demonstrated.

The angels all tried to block the onslaught with their shields. Most were successful, but some were badly burned. Those who had been severely injured suddenly turned into a ball of light and shot straight up in the air, diminishing as they soared above the cloud, and finally vanished in the darkness. All who were able promptly returned offensively with their swords, quickly penetrating the demons, and in several cases, severing limbs. As the demons were struck down, they fell to the ground, instantly transforming into liquid, pooling into a puddle of magma and then slowly seeping into the nearest channel of lava flow and disappearing.

The demons continued to utilize big rocks but stopped throwing them and instead used them to block the angels' swords. The fight continued as the Snyders and their traveling companions stood back and watched the epic battle, cheering the angels on as if they were spectators at an ancient Roman gladiator event and Raum's island was little more than an open coliseum.

~

Like her mother, Tatum couldn't help but think about the fact that the angels were wearing the identical armor they had been outfitted with in the past. They were out there physically fighting the same kind of battle that the Snyders, and the people who had been brave enough to take on the quest for home, had previously fought.

She began to consider the sixth chapter of the book of Ephesians. First the twelfth verse popped into her brain.

> For we do not wrestle against flesh and blood,
> but against the rulers, against the authorities,
> against the cosmic powers over this present

darkness, against the spiritual forces of evil in the heavenly places.

In that moment, the angels were fighting in place of the people they had created a barrier for. Tatum couldn't help but wonder how often this took place without people being aware of it. *We go about our everyday life completely clueless about how many dangers God rescues us from,* she told herself. As her mind pondered the thought, she also began to wonder how often the angels fight side by side with us, again, while we have no idea they are there or in any way involved with the battles we are facing. Gratefulness overwhelmed her heart, and she couldn't help but smile.

Her mind once again drifted to the sixth chapter of the book of Ephesians, but this time just a few verses further into it. She had long since connected the outfitting from the light to the belt of truth, breastplate of righteousness, gospel of peace, shield of faith, helmet of salvation, and the sword of the Spirit, the word of God, as described in that portion of the scriptures. The whole Snyder family had. Right then, however, watching that battle, she was not only captivated by the fact that the angels were dressed the same way they had been, but perhaps more importantly, how it made so much sense that the demons simply couldn't be.

~

The boys cheered loudly as the battle waged on. The angels went back and forth, and the numbers on both sides were steadily dwindling. Connor watched as one of the angels decapitated a demon, creating a small puddle of magma from the head and a larger one from the body. The small puddle merged with the larger one before the whole thing seeped into the nearest lava flow and disappeared like the others had.

Trevor saw an angel swing his sword at a demon and miss just before another demon blindsided him with a flame that covered his whole body. The angel immediately converted into a ball of light and ascended skyward. Trevor was relieved to watch a second angel stab the demon in the back, lift him over his head by the sword so that the demon's weight forced the sword all the way through his own body, then lowered him back down and used a foot to slide him off the sword where he, without delay, merged into the nearby lava stream.

Kinsey noticed that Raum was watching intently and consistently glanced up at the cloud. He wasn't sure if Raum was nervous, proud, or excited. Perhaps it was just another extension of his territorial nature. Regardless, while he had given up on trying to attack it, he was clearly preoccupied with the cloud. Rightfully so. The work the cloud was there to do was far from finished.

CHAPTER THIRTY-SEVEN
The Word

While the cheering hadn't totally subsided, it wasn't as aggressive as it had been in the beginning of the battle. The numbers of both angels and demons continued to dwindle, and Jill, among others, had begun to wonder if they would have to join the physical fight after all. Although the losses on both sides were happening in almost equal measure, when all was said and done, they still had Raum to contend with. It was a serious quandary that largely served to bring about additional wonderments.

Jill next considered the possibility that the cloud could still load them up with armor, and if they were going to have to face Raum, she certainly hoped that would happen. *Maybe the angels were just here to stop the other demons. We could still have to fight Raum ourselves,* she pondered. *That would make sense. It's what has happened before.*

She liked the idea of feeling the warmth that would come with the cloud again, as well as the powerful sensation that came wearing the armor, but the prospect of facing Raum for a third time was far from idyllic. What Jill was failing to take into account in that moment, however, was the fact that God rarely does things the way we expect.

~

Tatum looked on as an angel stabbed a demon in the shoulder, pinning him to the ground. Another demon struck the angel in the side of the head with a massive rock, causing him to let go of his sword and drop his shield.

A second angel on the men's side of the island sliced right through a demon's midsection, cutting him in half. As the demon puddled, he sprinted to help his fellow warrior. It had come down to these final two angels and the final two demons. But as he was hopping from rock to rock, avoiding lava flow, he and everyone else on the island witnessed the two demons simultaneously scorch the first angel he was rushing to rescue.

As the angel turned into a ball of light and ascended to Heaven, the only angel left leapt over a stream of lava and swung his sword, decapitating both demons in one fell swoop before landing on his feet to stand above the two puddles in victory.

~

The men cheered victoriously, but it was swiftly interrupted as they followed the angel's gaze to Raum who impulsively roared with ire. He was violently angry as he pounded his chest with furious intensity, wrathfully spewed fire into the air, and hastily stomped around his relatively small area, throwing a full-blown temper tantrum.

The angel looked on briefly but then turned his attention to the cloud. He extended a hand like one might do while inviting someone to join them and shouted, "Jehovah Sabaoth!"

The cloud suddenly began to gently descend. As it did, the light it was generating moved inward like a focusing flashlight, and the island slowly grew darker as a gentle, comforting breeze came with the cloud and touched everyone who watched.

Raum abruptly stopped throwing his tantrum, and instead of looking angry, seemed just as confused as everyone else at the cloud's unusual behavior. The Snyders had never seen this side of him before. He was making a lot of short grunting sounds as he continued to pace and glance around, often including brief looks at the cloud like he was checking its progress. His panic seemed to increase the closer the cloud came in its approach to the island, and it finally got the best of him.

~

The cloud was nearing ground level, and the light it was generating had formed a concentrated luminescence directly below it. Just before the cloud reached a full stop about fifty feet away from him, Raum freaked out and reacted by torching it with every bit of fire he could muster up and throw at it. The gentle breeze instantly vanished.

As the flames finally disappeared, so did the cloud, and the only sources of light were the flowing lava all over the island and the angel as he turned into another ball of light and ascended heavenward. Standing in the cloud's place, however, was a man. He was unharmed and appeared to be completely at peace.

Kinsey's eyes darted back and forth between the man and Raum who clearly recognized the person standing calmly before him. His panic immediately peaked, but it was no longer confusion or frustration he was showing. It was deep fear.

"Why are you here, Son of God?" Raum asked, frightfully backing away.

Raum's words immediately grabbed Kinsey's attention. He stared at the man who seemed to be starting to glow and suddenly recognized him, too. It was as if the Spirit inside of Kinsey leaped for joy. "Jesus," Kinsey cried out almost involuntarily, causing the boys around him to glance over at him before returning their gaze, eyes widening, to the Man standing before Raum.

The demon was cowering, even trembling. "What have you to do with any of this? Have you come just to torment me before the time?"

Jesus simply looked upon the demon with pity.

Raum suddenly raged like an animal backed into a corner. "This is my world! My dominion! What are you doing here, Son of God?"

The look of pity on Jesus' face didn't disappear, but it quickly merged with one of resolve as He dismissively waved His right hand at the demon. "Abadun." He spoke so softly hardly anyone could hear it.

But Raum did.

He tried to plead for mercy, but it was already too late. Just as the other demons had, Raum immediately turned into a puddle of magma and seeped into the lava flow between him and Jesus.

Raising both hands, Jesus looked up and spoke, "Yueid."

The island began to vibrate, and volcanic explosions from all over Kadosh were heard as the air filled with snow and ice that poured in from every direction, funneling into a steady stream and shooting straight down into the orb of lava in the middle of the island.

Every ounce of hot, liquid magma quickly cooled and hardened, creating a solid surface, and Jesus instantly became the only source of light on the island. "Mashelem," Jesus said with a satisfied smile.

Gazing at the majestic Person in front of them, everyone simultaneously bent their knees, pushed their left leg out behind them, placing their weight on its knee and their right foot. They folded their hands in front of them, closed their eyes, bowed their heads, and paid silent reverence to The Word of God.

Behind the people, the arctic terns landed on the perimeter of the island and stood with both the seals and the penguins who had climbed the embankment. Elsewhere, every created thing in Kadosh was joining them as they all bowed with the people before their maker and the true Lord over everything.

Jesus stretched out his arms and moved in a circle as He spoke, still softly, but somehow everyone both heard Him and understood what He was saying even though it was in a language no one there was familiar with. "Alnaas yatun."

The people all looked up to find that the light coming from Jesus had increased in its intensity. He had become a beacon in the middle of the island. They stood to their feet as the warm breeze the Snyders had felt before and longed for in its absence began to rush through the island once inhabited by Raum.

As they sprinted toward Jesus, the warmth everyone was

enjoying grew stronger. They circled around Him, simultaneously gathering with their loved ones. The joy pumping through the crowd was as palpable as the loving warmth emanating from their Savior. Jesus stepped forward and reached out, taking people by the hands, touching their shoulders and faces, greeting them by name, and offering all of them the most affectionate smile any of them had ever experienced.

As Jesus connected with each person, all the ailments they had been stricken with, from frostbite to simple muscle soreness, vanished in an instant. And shortly afterward, they disappeared from Kadosh forever.

He made His way around the circle, finally ending with the last four people on the island besides Himself. He hugged all four of them together. "Grant, Jill, Tatum, and Kinsey."

The warmth they experienced was the most incredible feeling any of them had ever taken in. No one wanted it to expire, but they took solace in the fact that they knew it was less of an ending and more of a pause. This feeling would come again, and they would spend the rest of their lives back home looking forward to the eternity they were going to be spending with Jesus.

"Well done, My good and faithful servants."

CHAPTER THIRTY-EIGHT
Return

    The Snyders sensed the warmth of Jesus beginning to fade before they heard the rushing sound or even realized that they had floated off the ground. The lasting effect of their encounter with Jesus was too joyful to leave room for any sadness, but they were quick to realize that they were most likely experiencing the trip, and all that came with it, for the last time on this side of Heaven. So, they opened themselves up as much as they possibly could to take in every bit of the splendor that the pulsating light and color surrounding them had to offer.

    Soon, their feet were once again softly touching down on the ground in the woods near their home. All the effort in the world couldn't have wiped the smiles off their faces. On the inside, their bodies tingled, and their hearts were full of love and gratitude, while on the outside the skin covering them remained warm. They were silent at first while they shared another group hug.

As they backed up, they realized that they were in their full winter getups again, exactly as they were when they left. They were even wearing the items they had given to other people.

"I guess I'm going to need to find a pair of scissors to get back out of these old, long underwear pants after all," Grant exclaimed, causing everyone to giggle before they turned to start sauntering home with a collective waddle.

After a few seconds of additional vocal silence, scored by the rhythmic "swish-swoosh" sound of the friction created by walking in their snow clothing, Jill decided she'd break it this time by raising the issue on everyone's mind. "Well, elephant in the room, or forest, or whatever the appropriate way to use that saying is at the moment…"

"Forest," Tatum responded. "Definitely forest."

"Elephant in the forest it is," Jill agreed before continuing. "This is where we need to hear confirmation from Kinsey that we just finished our last trip to Kadosh."

"That is what you said it would be," Grant added.

"I did," Kinsey agreed.

"Please don't add a 'but' to that," Tatum practically begged.

"No 'buts' or 'howevers,'" Kinsey stated with a hint of uncertainty in his voice.

"Thank God," Tatum said with a giant exhale.

"Why don't you sound more confident?" Grant asked skeptically.

"Well…" Kinsey started.

"Oh, no." Tatum's mitten-covered hand landed on her forehead with a puffy "thwack" sound.

"I should probably add a couple of qualifiers," Kinsey continued.

"Such as?" Jill asked, not sure if she wanted to hear the answer.

"I can say with confidence that we're done going to Kadosh as a foursome. We may even be done altogether. I'm just not a hundred percent sure."

"You mean we might have to go by ourselves?" Tatum practically yelled in exasperation. "That's even worse!"

"I don't know," Kinsey explained again. "I'm not saying we're going back at all. I'm just saying I can't be absolutely certain about that. But I am sure it's never going to happen again the way it has these last three times."

"That's not exactly the assurance I was looking for," Jill admitted.

"Yeah," Tatum agreed. "Ditto that!"

"Sorry," Kinsey said somewhat sheepishly.

"Not your fault," Grant reassured his son with a heavily

padded forearm-to-biceps smack. "That's one qualifier. You said you had a couple."

"Yeah," Kinsey admitted. "One more."

"Oh, great." Tatum exhaled deeply again.

"Like I said," Kinsey started, "we may very well be done with Kadosh."

"Right…" Jill coaxed.

Kinsey let out an exhale of his own as they started trying to waddle their way up the front steps to their house. "But we don't necessarily know that Kadosh is done with us."

"What the heck does that mean?" Tatum exclaimed as they all stopped on their porch and faced each other, three of them waiting for the explanation.

"Those angels and demons are waging war around us all the time even though we can't see them. We may not have to go to Raum next time. You never know. At some point, he may just come to us."

Kinsey opened the door and walked inside the house, leaving his parents and his sister staring at one another, wide-eyed and speechless.

Smoke was billowing out of a chimney on the rooftop of a nearby neighbor's house and a wisp suddenly formed a bird that sailed over the Snyders, completely unbeknownst to them, and then vanished into the forest.

The Four Corners of Winter

Kinsey was right, the spiritual world is always present.

The Four Corners of Winter

by C.S. Elston

The Four Corners of Winter

Reader's Guide

1. The Snyders share their experience to mixed reaction, causing them to hold it closer to the vest. How would you have handled it? Would you have shared it in the first place?

2. What do you think about the Peter Kreeft quote, "Thanksgiving comes after Christmas" that the Snyders hear in church?

3. Grant ponders the facts that the enemy can take something God intends for good and use it for evil and God can take something the enemy intends for evil and use it for good. What do you think about that? How does Genesis 50:20 influence your opinion. Do you have examples of either from your own life?

4. Grant went looking for other people who had experienced Kadosh and Raum. Is that something you would do? Why or why not?

5. When the Snyders ask if others they connect with would be willing to return to Kadosh with them, everyone refuses. How would you respond to such a request?

6. Shortly after arriving in Kadosh, Tatum realizes she might need to figure out how to make snowshoes, and the people the Snyders encounter have all figured out how to build fires. If you were in a similar situation, what kind of survival skills do you possess that would come in handy?

7. Most of the people trapped in Kadosh don't put up as big of a fight this time around, when it comes to joining the Snyders on the quest to escape. How easy or difficult would that decision be for you?

Reader's Guide

8. Grant believes that people tend to think of God as slow when He is really showing patience and Jill explains that she doesn't want to leave a single person behind and that the One who sent her doesn't either. How are these ideas related and what light does 2 Peter 3:9 shed on the subject?

9. Hoshi says, "Some people will never give up their right to make bad decisions no matter how much time we give them." Can you think of any examples that point to the truth of this statement?

10. Irisa agreed that trying to convince people to join the quest was the right thing to do, but didn't expect anyone to change their mind. Have you ever felt obligated to do something but didn't expect the results to be positive?

11. During their run-in with the smoke spiders, Tatum states that she thinks Raum sends obstacles like those to try and convince people to give up. Do you ever feel like Satan uses a similar tactic, placing obstacles in or path in an attempt to cause us to give up on something God wants us to pursue?

12. Kinsey considered it failure to leave anyone behind and the frustration of that reality nagged at him in a persistent and "annoying" way. How do you react to failure?

13. When the men are lost in the forest of ice spires, Grant prays and trusts God even though he can't see a way out and has no idea how God will help them. Can you think of a relatable moment in your life?

14. Connor tells Kinsey he'll be okay if he never sees snow again while Kinsey likes the snow. How do you feel about it? What's the worst kind of weather you can imagine being trapped in with no end in sight?

15. When the spirits from beneath the ice surface and try to join the journey, the fire from within the cloud burns brightly and the spirits respond in two very different ways. How is this like the human response to God, and how is the result like our own eternal fate?

16. When they reach Raum's island, Kinsey thinks back on the book of Psalms and ponders the idea that "there is no place we can go where God is not already there." Do you agree? What does this idea mean to you?

17. The cloud hovers above Raum's island and doesn't descend all the way to outfit people for battle like it did in the first two books. The Snyders maintain their faith in God while not being able to figure out how His help will come. Have you ever been in a relatable situation? If so, how difficult was it for you to maintain your own faith?

18. Tatum considers the notion that we have no idea how many dangers God rescues us from in our everyday lives. How should this concept affect our attitudes that tend toward grumbling and griping?

19. What do you think about the fact that Jesus exercises so much power by calmly speaking a word?

20. Kinsey raises the possibility that Raum could show up back home. What do you think about this and what do you think the future looks like for the Snyders?

Also by C.S. Elston

Now Available:

"The Four Corners"

"The Four Corners of Darkness"

"The Gift of Tyler"

"The Gift of Rio"

Coming Soon:

"The Gift of Matias"

"The Gift of Amanda"

After award-winning stage work in the nineties, Chris Elston moved to Los Angeles where he wrote more than two dozen feature film and television screenplays. He has been invited to participate in screenwriting events for Cinema Seattle and Angel Citi Film Festival. In 2013, Chris left Los Angeles for the suburbs of his hometown, Seattle, Washington, to get married and start a new chapter in his own story. The journey of the chapter that followed eventually landed he and his wife in Northern Arizona where they now reside.

www.ingramcontent.com/pod-product-compliance
Ingram Content Group UK Ltd.
Pitfield, Milton Keynes, MK11 3LW, UK
UKHW042157171224
452513UK00001B/169